PERCEPTIONS

a selection of modern English writing

edited by

SHANTA RAMESHWAR RAO

LOWER PRICED SPECIAL STUDENTS EDITION

Orient Longman

Cover design: Arputharani Sengupta

PERCEPTIONS

ORIENT LONGMAN PRIVATE LIMITED

Registered Office
3-6-752 Himayatnagar, Hyderabad 500 029 (A.P.), INDIA

Other Offices
Bangalore, Bhopal, Bhubaneshwar, Chennai, Ernakulam, Guwahati, Hyderabad, Jaipur, Kolkata, Lucknow, Mumbai, New Delhi, Patna

First published 1988
Reprinted 1990, 1992, 1993, 1994, 1995, 1998, 1999, 2000,
2002 (twice), 2003 2004

ISBN 81 250 0640 0

Phototypeseting by
Avittam
Chennai

Printed in india by
Beekay offset press
Chennai 600 013

Published by
Orient Longman Private Ltd.
160 Anna Salai
Chennai 600 002

I would like to thank Theresa Francis for her speedy and efficient typing of the material in this anthology and Eleanor Watts for going over the texts and making many valuable suggestions.

SHANTA RAMESHWAR RAO

Introduction

This anthology features a selection of modern prose drawn mainly from books and serious journalistic writing. The underlying theme is people — men, women, children — in a variety of encounters with the world around them. The nucleus of experience in each piece of text is different: from *The Night the Policemen Came* and *A Night with the Bears* which deal with being pitted against power to *My Muscles Froze*, which is about fear, and *Ziré Buzette* which deals light-heartedly with death.

The purpose in each case has been to project human experience on two levels — as situations which are familiar or of interest to young people, and by way of creating an *awareness* of the issues that confront us today. *A Different Kind of Learning* is thus about the limitations of education-by-rote, and *The Election* about oppression and injustice.

Humour has also influenced the selection of several texts in the anthology as has the editor's interest in projecting writing mostly from or about people in India and other non-European cultures.

The exercises following each piece of text are intended to help the student gain global comprehension of the material as well as an understanding of specific aspects of it. The vocabulary exercises, involving matching, transformation and extension aim to build on the student's word-store.

The editor intends the texts in this anthology to be used in a variety of ways to develop the skills of reading, writing, listening and discussion.

Contents

Acknowledgements

For permission to use copyright material the editor and publishers are grateful to India Book House Pvt. Ltd., Bombay, for *Pret in the House* from 'A Haunting he would go' by Ruskin Bond; Oxford University Press, New Delhi, for *I Prepare to go to Coimbatore* from 'Climbing the coconut tree' by Kasturi Sreenivasan; John Farquaharson Ltd., London, for *My Muscles Froze* from 'Black Boy' by Richard Wright; Jonathan Clowes Limited, London, on behalf of Doris Lessing for *No Witchcraft for Sale* from 'This was the old chief's country' by Doris Lessing; India Book House Pvt. Ltd., Bombay, for *The Night the Policeman Came* from 'The Narayanpur incident' by Sashi Deshpande; J.S. Wong and Curtis Brown Ltd., New York, for *A Different Kind of Learning* from 'Fifth Chinese daughter' by Jade Snow Wong; Hans Peter Richter, Edite Kroll, Penguin Books Ltd., London, and Longman Young Books, London, for *The Election* from 'I was there' by Hans Peter Richter; Macdonald, London, for *The Tunguska Event and The Comets* from 'Cosmos' by Carl Sagan.

Every attempt has been made to trace holders of copyright. The publishers would appreciate such information from those not listed here, as would enable them to make appropriate acknowledgements in future editions of this book.

The publishers have been unable to identify the source of Zire' Buzette by Maurice des Ombriaux.

PROSE

1. Pret in the House

It was Grandmother who decided that we must move to another house. And it was all because of a pret, a mischievous ghost, who had been making life intolerable for everyone.

In India, prets usually live in peepal trees, and that's where our Pret first had his abode — in the branches of an old peepal which had grown through the compound wall and had spread into the garden on our side, and over the road on the other side.

For many years the Pret had lived there quite happily, without bothering anyone in the house. I suppose the traffic on the road had kept him fully occupied. Sometimes, when a tonga was passing, he would frighten the pony, and as a result the little pony-cart would go careening off in the wrong direction. Occasionally he would get into the engine of a car or bus, which would soon afterwards have a breakdown. And he liked to knock the sola-topis off the heads of sahibs, who would curse and wonder how a breeze had sprung up so suddenly, only to die down again just as quickly. Although the Pret could make himself felt, and sometimes heard, he was invisible to the human eye.

At night people avoided walking beneath the peepal tree. It was said that if you yawned beneath the tree, the Pret would jump down your throat and ruin your digestion. Grandmother's tailor, Jaspal, who never had anything ready on time, blamed the Pret for all his troubles. Once, when yawning, Jaspal had forgotten to snap his fingers in front of his mouth — always mandatory when yawning beneath peepal trees — and the Pret had got in without any difficulty. Since then, Jaspal had always been suffering from tummy upsets.

But it had left our family alone until, one day, the peepal tree had been cut down.

It was nobody's fault except, of course, that Grandfather had given the PWD permission to cut the tree, which had been on our land. They wanted to widen the road, and the tree and a bit of wall were in the way; so both had to go. In any case, not even a ghost can prevail against the Public Works Department. But hardly a day had passed when we discovered that the Pret, deprived of his tree, had decided to take up residence in the bungalow. And since a good Pret must be bad in order to justify his existence, he was soon up to all sorts of mischief in the house.

He began by hiding Grandmother's spectacles whenever she took them off.

'I'm sure I put them down on the dressing-table,' she grumbled.

A little later they were found balanced precariously on the snout of a wild boar, whose stuffed and mounted head adorned the verandah wall. Being the only boy in the house, I was at first blamed for this prank; but a day or two later, when the spectacles disappeared again only to be discovered dangling from the wires of the parrot's cage, it was agreed that some other agency was at work.

Grandfather was the next to be troubled. He went into the garden one morning to find all his prize sweet-peas snipped off and lying on the ground.

Uncle Ken was the next to suffer. He was a heavy sleeper, and once he'd gone to bed he hated being woken up. So when he came to the breakfast table looking bleary-eyed and miserable, we asked if he was feeling all right.

'I couldn't sleep a wink last night,' he complained. 'Every time I was about to fall asleep, the bedclothes would be pulled off the bed. I had to get up at least a dozen times to pick them off the floor.' He stared balefully at me. 'Where were you sleeping last night, young man?'

I had an alibi. 'In Grandfather's room,' I said.

'That's right,' said Grandfather. 'And I'm a light sleeper. I'd have woken up if he'd been sleep-walking.'

'It's that ghost from the peepal tree,' said Grandmother. 'It's moved into the house. First my spectacles, then the sweet-peas, and now Ken's bedclothes! What will it be up to next, I wonder?'

We did not have to wonder long. There followed a series of disasters. Vases fell off tables, pictures fell from walls. Parrot's feathers turned up in the teapot, while the parrot himself let out indignant squawks in the middle of the night. Uncle Ken found a crow's nest in his bed, and on tossing it out of the window was attacked by two crows.

When Aunt Minnie came to stay, things got worse. The Pret seemed to take an immediate dislike to Aunt Minnie. She was a nervous, excitable person, just the right sort of prey for a spiteful ghost. Somehow her toothpaste got switched with a tube of Grandfather's shaving-cream, and when she appeared in the sitting-room, foaming at the mouth, we ran for our lives, Unlce Ken shouting that she'd got rabies.

Two days later Aunt Minnie complained that she had been hit on the nose by a grapefruit, which had of its own accord taken a leap from the pantry shelf and hurtled across the room straight at her. A bruised and swollen nose testified to the attack. Aunt Minnie swore that life had been more peaceful in upper Burma.

'We'll have to leave this house,' declared Grandmother. 'If we stay here much longer, both Ken and Minnie will have nervous breakdowns.'

'I thought Aunt Minnie broke down long ago,' I said.

'None of your cheek!' snapped Aunt Minnie.

'Anyway, I agree about changing the house,' I said breezily. 'I can't even do my homework. The ink-bottle is always empty.'

'There was ink in the soup last night,' complained Grandfather.

And so, a few days and several disasters later, we began moving to a new house.

Two bullock-carts laden with furniture and heavy luggage were sent ahead. The roof of the old car was piled high with bags and kitchen utensils. Everyone squeezed into the car, and Grandfather took the driver's seat.

We were barely out of the gate when we heard a peculiar sound, as if someone was chuckling and talking to himself on the roof of the car.

'Is the parrot out there on the luggage-rack?' asked Grandfather.

'No, he's in his cage on a bullock-cart,' said Grandmother.

Grandfather stopped the car, got out, and took a look at the roof.

'Nothing up there,' he said, getting in again and starting the engine. 'I'm sure I heard the parrot talking.'

Grandfather had driven some way up the road when the chuckling started again, followed by a squeaky little voice. We all heard it. It was the Pret talking to itself.

'Let's go, let's go!' it squeaked gleefully. 'A new house, I can't wait to see it. What fun we're going to have!'

(from *Ghosts of a Hill-Station* by Ruskin Bond)

Glossary

abode :	home
careen :	to go forward tilting to one side
sola topi :	a hat that the British wore as protection against the sun
mandatory :	by official order; compulsory
to prevail against :	to win a fight against
precarious :	unsafe; not firm or steady
prank :	a playful but foolish practical joke or trick
snout :	the long nose of some animals such as pigs
sweet pea :	a kind of sweet-scented flower
snip :	short, quick cut with scissors
bleary-eyed :	with eyes that are red and unable to see well because of tiredness, lack of sleep, tears, etc.
baleful :	evil; full of hate
alibi :	the plea or excuse of having been somewhere else when a crime was committed
switched :	exchanged
of its own accord :	willingly; without being forced
Aunt Minnie's Swollen nose testified to the attack :	was proof of the attack
none of your cheek :	none of your impudence; don't be rude
laden with :	loaded with
barely out of the gate :	hardly out of the gate

Vocabulary

A. *From each set of words find the word or phrase that means the same as the first one.*

glee : mischief, anger, fear, mirth, foolishness, stupidity.

dangling . clanging loudly, ringing musically, hanging loosely, clinging tightly, singing melodiously.

miserable : high-spirited, unhappy, merry, talkative, silent, grumpy.

series of : many of, a succession of, plenty of, none of, very few of.

occasionally : often, once a month, somewhere, sometimes, every Tuesday, once a fortnight.

leap : writhe, jump, skip, hop, step, dance, turn.

adorn : celebrate, adore, beautify, change, worship.

bothering : needing, touching, troubling, injuring, frightening.

B. *Fill in the blanks below. The first one is done for you.*

What cannot be
1. heard is inaudible.
2. seen is __________.
3. described is __________.
4. tolerated is __________.
5. escaped is __________.
6. excused is __________.

C. *In each set of words below tick off the one which doesn't belong and say why you think it doesn't belong. (Consult a dictionary if necessary.)*

1. nervous, kind-hearted, foolishly, hardworking, excitable.
2. barking, mewing, howling, braying, neighing, galloping.
3. mother, uncle, nephew, niece, generation, aunt.
4. ghost, haunt, spirit, spectre, wraith.
5. leaves, branches, trunk, bark, roots, creeper.

D. *Each of the following prefixes may be added to a word to form its opposite:*

un-	*in-*	*im-*	*il-*	*anti-*	*dis-*

Choose the correct prefix to form the opposite of these words:

please	polite	legal	personal	formal
excusable	legible	social	agreeable	cultured
conscious	auspicious	lucky	mature	proper
national	frequent	used	heartened	logical
active				

Comprehension

A. *Choose the correct ending to the sentences.*

1. For a long time the pret didn't bother anyone in the house because he
   a. had his hands full, frightening ponies on the road.
   b. was far too busy knocking sola-topis off the heads of sahibs.
   c. was busy playing his pranks and didn't care.
   d. was busy playing his tricks on the traffic in the road.
2. People could
   a. hear the pret but couldn't feel his presence.
   b. feel his presence and hear his voice but couldn't see him.
   c. see him but couldn't hear him.
   d. hear him and see him and even feel his presence.
3. The pret
   a. jumped down the tailor's throat and spoilt his digestion.
   b. forgot to snap his fingers in front of his mouth when he yawned.
   c. didn't yawn when he snapped his fingers in front of his mouth.
   d. never had anything ready on time.
4. For many years the pret
   a. had lived in the peepal tree which belonged to the writer's family.
   b. lived quietly on the road outside the compound wall.
   c. was needed for widening the road.
   d. fought a war with the Public Works Department.
5. According to the writer a pret is good only if he
   a. hides Grandmother's spectacles.
   b. is wicked and mischievous.

a. can win the fight against the Public Works Department.
d. makes his home in a peepal tree.

6. The pret first came into the house because
   a. his job was to haunt it.
   b. he was tired of living in the open.
   c. he was left without a home when the peepal tree was cut down.
   d. he had frequent stomach upsets and a bad digestion.
7. Grandmother blamed the pret for
   a. all the disasters.
   b. attacking the crows outside the window.
   c. disturbing Uncle Ken's sweet-peas.
   d. disliking Aunt Minnie.
8. Aunt Minnie
   a. had rabies, poor thing.
   b. ate a grapefruit in the pantry.
   c. used bad language and swore.
   d. used Grandmother's shaving cream to brush her teeth.

B. *Mark the true statements T, the false ones F and the ones about which the text does not say anything DS. Correct the false ones if you can.*

1. There is a suggestion in the story that Aunt Minnie had once lived in Upper Burma.
2. The family in the story were tired of the pret's pranks, so they decided to move into another house.
3. Uncle Ken took the decision to move into another house.
4. Grandfather grew flowers in the garden.
5. Uncle Ken had a nervous breakdown.
6. The pret went with the family to their new house riding on the roof of their car.
7. The spectacles belonged to Grandmother and they were found on the snout of the stuffed and mounted head of the wild boar.
8. Aunt Minnie came into the sitting room foaming at the mouth because the pret had exchanged her toothpaste with father's shaving cream.
9. The pret was responsible for a series of disasters in the house.
10. The family had a parrot.
11. Many stuffed and mounted animal heads adorned the verandah walls of the haunted house.
12. While in the car, Grandfather mistook the parrot's voice for the pret's.

2. I Prepare to go to Coimbatore

Kasturi Sreenivasan's 'Climbing the Coconut Tree' from which this passage is taken starts with a quotation:

> How far can you support a man climbing a coconut tree?
> Only as far as your hand can reach; after that, he has to
> do the climbing himself.

The author calls his book 'a partial autobiography'.

Ever since I started to learn English, I had known that I would have to go to school in Coimbatore. It had never struck me to question that decision. I was not trained to question things, but merely to accept them as they were. Coimbatore was only twenty miles away. My father would be coming at least once a month and I would spend the holidays in the village. And my aunt would be there to look after me. Yet I was miserable. My whole world was circumscribed within the limits of the village. The occasional forays into the outer world were excursions into the unknown. I was glad to return to the safety and security of my own world. To leave such a world was a great sorrow, to leave all my friends and my old haunts behind. I wondered if they would still be the same when I came back. I remember thinking that even the trees would have grown taller by the time I returned (it never struck me that I too would grow taller or change). I remember breaking the branches of a tree and thinking to myself, 'at least this stump will remain a stump until I come back.' I went round the village looking at things, trying to memorise them, to fix them in my heart so that at least in my memory they would remain constant, without change. I hid little useless objects in various unlikely corners in the hope that they would still be there when I came back. If these remained undisturbed in my absence, it was a source of elation. My mother was my only informant on these matters and when I asked her once about an old notebook, she replied without understanding, 'It must have been thrown away when we did the annual cleaning a few months ago.' How callous could people be?

An auspicious day was chosen for my departure and during the last few days, everything naturally revolved round me. My mother made my favourite dishes, almost everybody talked about the promised high school career, friends came to say good-bye, the few clothes I had were put together and I was assured I would have new ones as soon as I got to Coimbatore. I hoped that these would be suitable to my status as a high school student. My aunt and the servant had already left to get the house ready for my arrival.

On the morning of my departure, a few of the uncles came to see me off. The horse cart was got ready and I touched Grandfather's feet to say good-bye to him. I had always thought of him as an eternal fixture in the house. Little did I realise that I would not see him alive again. He was now eighty-five, very frail and totally blind. But he got to his feet, shuffled slowly to the room where his safe was kept, opened it, took out a currency note and asked me, 'What is it?'

'A hundred-rupee note, Grandfather,' I replied.

'It is too much,' he said and put it back. He got out a ten-rupee note and handed it to me. 'I want you to be a four-sleeved lawyer when you grow up,' he blessed me.

'Grandfather is careful with money as usual,' the family members sniggered, and we set off.

Grandfather's deserving charity

For as long as I had known him, Grandfather had intended to spend some money on charity. 'God has been good to me,' he would say to whoever cared to listen. 'My children are well off in life. So why shouldn't I give away something to a highly deserving charity?'

But Grandmother, who knew, was highly sceptical of his intentions. 'He has never given anything away in his life and I don't think he will start now,' she said.

If one of the fifteen uncles happened to be listening, he would say, 'Yes, you can certainly afford to do it.'

'The only question is, which charity?' Grandfather would ask. 'Or even more important, to whom? It is difficult to give to a charity without it benefiting someone else at the same time.'

Education, medical relief, building a choultry, building a new gopuram to our temple, were all suggested to him at various times by different people. But he had objections to each suggestion on the grounds that it might help someone undeserving of his munificence! School teachers would merely hoodwink him and spend the money on something else; so education was out. He had lived without taking any medicine in his whole life, and why should other people not do the same? So medical relief could not be considered. Temple priests attracted his wrath more than anyone else, so the temple had to get on without a new gopuram. A choultry was a place where a whole lot of lazy, good-for-nothing people got together to gossip and perhaps smoke opium! Innocent and unsuspecting people having heard of his intention, approached Grandfather, hoping that perhaps they might be the lucky ones to get a large donation out of him for some worthy cause. But they soon learnt how unworthy their causes were, how selfish they were in approaching him and how dull to imagine him a fool!

But as Grandfather became increasingly feeble and as the end undeniably approached, my father took the matter in hand. He told the old gentleman that he should make up his mind soon, and that any charity was better than no charity. Grandfather confessed, 'I have never hesitated to take decisions in my life; but this decision I find impossible. You had better do something after I am gone.'

One of the things that was obligatory for a prosperous Hindu was 'godhan', the gift of a cow to a holy Brahmin before his final departure from this world. It was supposed to ensure smooth passage into heaven for the donor and Grandfather was persuaded somewhat reluctantly to perform at least this charity. On the day of the ceremony, when all the preliminaries were completed, he wanted to know how much milk the cow was likely to give. On being told, he said, 'That is too much. I don't need that much milk, neither does this Brahmin. Couldn't you find something a little less expensive?'

When, finally, he agreed to give away the cow, instead of meekly receiving the blessing from the Brahmin, he admonished him. 'Look after the cow properly, swami. Don't forget that this cow has to take care of you in this world and me in the next.'

When he died, there was a large amount of money in the safe as well as a note asking my father to spend it on charity, 'which I have been unable to do'.

(from *Climbing the Coconut Tree* by Kasturi Sreenivasan)

Glossary

circumscribed : to draw a line around; to mark the boundary of; to set limits to

forays : raids to get food, capture booty, etc.

old haunts : places which used to be frequently visited

callous : indifferent to the pain or distress of others

frail : delicate; easily damaged or destroyed

snigger : to laugh in a sly, half-suppressed manner
sceptical : doubtful about the truth of anything — especially of what others say
choultry : a free guest house for travellers
gopuram : the pyramid-shaped roof of a South Indian Hindu temple
munificence : generosity; lavishness; extravagance
admonish : to scold mildly

A. *A new word can be formed by joining two words together. Such words are called compound words. The compound is either written as a single word, or with a hypen joining the two words or even as two seperate words.*

Match the words in Box A to those in Box B. Use these compound words to fill in the sentences below.

Box A	Box B
bird	dressed
well	book
dimly	case
note	behaved
tax	mown
badly	watcher
well	natured
ill	equipped
good	lit
newly	mannered
brief	payers

1. Anita never forgets to greet people when she meets them or to thank them when they give her something. She's a very ______________ child.
2. Those shabby sandals, those torn trousers, the frayed collar and sleeves! Why are you so ______________ , Sudhir?
3. Javed is entitled to vote because he pays his taxes. All ______________ are entitled to vote.
4. My aunt is an enthusiastic ______________ . She's always watching birds through her binoculars out in the garden.

5. You need a book in which to take down your notes. A ____________ is what you want.
6. The child behaves very well. He's a gentle ____________ boy.
7. The room has hardly any light. It's a very ____________ room.
8. The grass in this lawn was mown only this morning. You can see that the lawn has been ____________.

B. *The suffix–**ify** is used when something becomes or is caused to become something else.*

He tried to <u>justify</u> what he had done.

*Fill in the blank in sentence <u>b</u> with an–**ify** word so that it means the same as the underlined word/phrase in sentence <u>a</u>.*

1. a. The language you've used in this story is too difficult. I wish you would make it <u>simple.</u>
   b. I wish you would ____________ it.
2. a. Here are some pictures of the people in the story. Can you <u>tell the identity</u> of each?
   b. Can you ____________ each one?
3. a. The appearance of the white veiled figure night after night puzzled us. It <u>was a mystery</u> to us.
   b. The appearance of the white veiled figure night after night ____________ us.
4. a. The nouns, verbs, adjectives and adverbs in Box A are all jumbled up. The student's task is to <u>put them into classes</u> under different heads.
   b. The student's task is to ____________ them under different heads.
5. a. The three-headed dragon struck <u>terror</u> in the hearts of the children.
   b. The three-headed dragon ____________ the children.
6. a. You must add a lot of water to this powder and <u>make it into a liquid.</u>
   b. You must add a lot of water to this powder and ____________ it.

Comprehension

A. *Tick off the correct ending to the sentences below:*

1. Grandfather had every intention of giving money to a deserving charity but when it came to action, he
   a. made a totally wrong decision.
   b. found he had no money at all to give.
   c. found his sons wouldn't allow him to give away any money.
   d. made all sorts of excuses not to give it.
2. The old man had made
   a. a will asking his son to give away his money to whatever charity he thought worthy.
   b. a testament leaving his wealth to all his grandchildren.
   c. provision for his wife.
   d. his sons pay the villagers what he owed them.
3. Before he died a wealthy Hindu was expected to
   a. give a cow in charity to a worthy cause.
   b. spend his money for holy purposes.
   c. gift a cow to a Brahmin.
   d. feed all the poor in his neighbourhood.
4. In all his life Grandfather had never
   a. spoken ill of anyone.
   b. taken any medicine.
   c. told the truth.
   d. hoodwinked people.
5. As the end approached Grandfather seemed quite willing
   a. to die.
   b. to perform religious ceremonies.
   c. to leave the question of charity to his son.
   d. to make a deed transferring his property to his son's name.
6. Many people came to Grandfather hoping
   a. to get his blessings.
   b. to make him understand their problems.
   c. to cheat him out of some money.
   d. to get money from him for a worthy cause.
7. When people came to Grandfather for money
   a. he never refused them.
   b. sent them away empty handed.

c. told them he would think about it.
d. asked them to wait until he died.

8. The writer seems
   a. unhappy about his Grandfather's stupidity.
   b. rather amused by the old man's miserliness.
   c. angry about his grandparents' quarrels.
   d. ashamed of his Grandmother's old fashioned attitudes.
9. Perhaps the only gift Grandfather had ever made in his life was
   a. land.
   b. the cow.
   c. money for a temple.
   d. old clothes.
10. Grandmother was very doubtful that
    a. her husband would outlive her.
    b. her sons would obey their father.
    c. the old man would take medicine and get well.
    d. he would give money to charity at this late stage in his life.

B. *Mark the true statements T, the false ones F and the ones about which the text does not say anything DS. Correct the false ones.*

1. Grandmother was a shrewd woman and knew her husband well.
2. Grandmother was blunt and outspoken.
3. Gradmother lived in constant fear of her husband.
4. Grandmother gave large amounts of money in charity.
5. The writer loved money as much as his grandfather did.
6. Grandfather told everyone that they didn't deserve to get any of his money.
7. Everyone told Grandfather he should not be stingy.
8. The writer studied Tamil and English.
9. In the end the writer's grandfather decided to gift a cow to a Brahmin.
10. Grandfather believed that gifting a cow would make it easy for him to go to heaven.
11. School teachers hoodwinked Grandfather.
12. A choultry is a place where a lot of good-for-nothing people get together to gossip and perhaps smoke opium.

C. *Find the lines in the text which mean the same as those given below.*

1. It was my habit never to ask my elders the reason for their actions. I had been brought up to obey them implicity without understanding.
2. I kept all sorts of things in corners where no one would notice them, hoping that they would still be there, exactly as they were, when I came back.
3. It made me very happy if the objects I had hidden away stayed as they were, unseen and untouched by others.
4. I never realised that I would grow and change.
5. I had believed that Grandfather was permanent, and would always be in the house.
6. The village was my entire world.
7. When I did go out of the village sometimes, those trips were like adventures into strange places nobody knew about.
8. The only person I shared my thoughts with was my mother.

3. My Muscles Froze

Most of us know what it means to feel shy or embarrassed in the presence of a large number of people. In the passage below, taken from Richard Wright's autobiography, 'Black Boy', the author describes his first day at school.

But I was still shy and half paralysed when in the presence of a crowd, and my first day at the new school made me the laughing stock of the classroom. I was sent to the blackboard to write my name and address; I knew my name and address, knew how to write it, knew how to spell it; but standing at the blackboard with the eyes of the many girls and boys looking at my back made me freeze inside and I was unable to write a single letter.

'Write your name,' the teacher called to me.

I lifted the white chalk to the blackboard and, as I was about to write, my mind went blank, empty; I could not remember my name, not even the first letter. Somebody giggled and I stiffened.

'Just forget us and write your name and address,' the teacher coaxed. An impulse to write would flash through me, but my hand would refuse to move. The children began to titter and I flushed hotly.

'Don't you know your name?' the teacher asked.

I looked at her and could not answer. The teacher rose and walked to my side, smiling at me to give me confidence. She placed her hand tenderly upon my shoulder.

'What's your name?' she asked.

'Richard,' I whispered.

'Richard what?'

'Richard Wright.'

'Spell it.'

I spelled my name in a wild rush of letters, trying desperately to redeem my paralysing shyness.

'Spell it slowly so that I can hear it,' she directed me.

I did.

'Now can you write?'

'Yes, ma'am.'

'Then write it.'

Again I turned to the blackboard and lifted my hand to write, then I was blank and void within. I tried frantically to collect my senses but I could remember nothing. A sense of the girls and boys behind me filled me to the exclusion of everything. I realised how utterly I was failing and I grew weak and leaned my hot forehead against the cold blackboard. The room burst into a loud and prolonged laugh and my muscles froze.

'You may go to your seat,' the teacher said.

I sat and cursed myself. Why did I always appear so dumb when I was called to perform something in a crowd? I knew how to write as well as any pupil in the classroom, and no doubt I could read better than any of them, and I could talk fluently and expressively when I was sure of myself. Then why did strange faces make me freeze? I sat with my ears and neck burning, hearing the pupils whisper about me, hating myself, hating them.

(from *Black Boy* by Richard Wright)

Vocabulary

A. *From the list in the box choose three words that describe each of the following people in Richard Wright's story.*

1. The teacher   2. The children   3. The boy

harsh	*excitable*	*pompous*	*crazy*
kindly	*cunning*	*greedy*	*arrogant*
unkind	*miserly*	*miserable*	*frightened*
unhappy	*encouraging*	*amused*	*ridiculous*
paralytic	*unsympathetic*	*friendly*	*unfriendly*
wise	*nervous*	*unintelligent*	*sympathetic*

B. *In each set of words given below there is one that does not belong. Which is it? Can you explain why it doesn't belong?*

1. smile, giggle, titter, laugh, grin, exclaim, chuckle.
2. silent, blank, empty, vacant, void.
3. panic-striken, frantic, stupid, desperate.
4. hate, detest, loathe, dislike, angry.
5. gently, tenderly, fluently, softly.
6. mumble, talk, whisper, lisp, chatter, stroll, speak, mutter.

C. *All the verbs in the passage below have been substituted with the word* ***bonk.*** *The* ***bonk*** *words have been used in their correct grammatical forms ('ed' for the past tense, 'ing' for the present participle, etc.). There will of course not be any one correct word to fill into the place of the* ***bonk*** *word: there will be alternatives. Here is a hint to help you:*

> The first *bonk* could stand for any of these words:
> *arrived, walked, ran, came, crept, crawled, fled, galloped etc.*

You will need to decide which of these words would be the best in the sentence.

An elder sister *bonked* from the town to *bonk* a younger one. The elder one was *bonked* to a tradesman, and the younger to a peasant. As the two *bonked* tea and *bonked*, the elder sister began to *bonk* about her life in town — how she *bonked* in ease and comfort, *bonked* after her children well, *bonked* nice things to *bonk* and *bonk* and *bonked bonking* and *bonking* to the theatre.

Comprehension

A. *Choose the correct endings to the sentences below.*

1. The boy in the story was unable to write a single letter though
   a. he was half-paralysed.
   b. he knew how to write and spell.
   c. the other children laughed at him.
   d. he was in the presence of a crowd.
2. The teacher smiled and placed her hand tenderly on him to
   a. make him read.
   b. make him freeze.
   c. give him confidence.
   d. make him talk fluently.
3. The boy was not stupid. He could talk fluently and expressively when he was
   a. paralysed.
   b. the laughing stock of the classroom.
   c. blank and void within.
   d. sure of himself.
4. The boy hated himself because
   a. the children laughed at him.
   b. he was stupid.
   c. he appeared stupid.
   d. he was weak.
5. The boy was so shy that
   a. he couldn't see what was before him.
   b. his hand wouldn't move.
   c. he cursed himself.
   d. he could read better than any of them.

Composition

Can you remember a time when you were very angry with a friend because you had misunderstood something she or he had said or done?

— Describe how the misunderstanding came about.
— Say how you discovered that it was a misunderstanding.
— Say what you did when you realised that you had been wrong.
— And finally, say what your friend said or did after that.

4. No Witchcraft for Sale

'No Witchcraft for Sale' is a story that looks at the relationship between the black African and the white settler in Southern Rhodesia. It is about the Farquars who had a large farm, and Gideon, their cook. The Farquars had been childless for many years. When little Teddy was born their servants rejoiced greatly. Gideon was the closest to the baby and called him 'Little Yellow Head'.

Gideon had been with the Farquars for many years. He and Teddy were great friends from the first. When Gideon had finished his work, he would lift Teddy on his shoulders to the shade of a big tree, and play with him there, making him toys from twigs and leaves and grass, or shaping animals from wetted soil. When Teddy learned to walk, Gideon would crouch before him, clucking encouragement, finally catching him when he fell, tossing him up in the air till they both became breathless with laughter. Mrs Farquar was fond of the the old cook because of his love for the child.

Gideon stayed on the farm with his family. Sometimes his own small child, born at the same time as Teddy, would peer at Teddy from a distance and stare at his fair hair and blue eyes. The two children would gaze at each other, and once Teddy put out his hand curiously to touch the black child's cheeks and hair.

'Ah Missus,' said Gideon, who was watching, 'these are both children, and one will grow up to be a Baas, and one will be a servant' and Mrs Farquar smiled and said sadly: 'Yes Gideon, I was thinking the same.' 'It is God's will,' Gideon would sigh, and Mrs Farquar would agree.

As time passed a change seemed to be coming into their lives. Gideon continued to be kind, but he became increasingly distant and formal, not because of resentment, but in the way a person accepts something inevitable. Teddy's manner also changed. He began to talk to Gideon more and more in the way a white man talks to a servant, expecting to be obeyed.

One day Teddy came staggering into the kitchen with his fists to his eyes, shrieking with pain. Gideon dropped the hot pot of soup he was holding, rushed to the child and forced aside his fingers. 'A snake!', he exclaimed. A tree-snake, hanging by its tail from the roof, had spat full in the boy's eyes. Mrs Farquar came running. 'He'll go blind, Gideon,' she sobbed, holding Teddy close to her. Already the eyes, with perhaps half an hour's sight left in them, were swollen up to the size of fists, and Teddy's face was distorted by great purple oozing protuberances. Gideon said, 'Wait a minute, Missus, I'll get some medicine.' He ran off into the bush.

Mrs Farquar bathed the child's eyes with permanganate. She stood by the window, holding the little boy in her arms and peered helplessly into the bush. In a few minutes Gideon came bounding back, a plant in his hand.

'Do not be afraid, Missus,' said Gideon, 'this will cure Little Yellow Head's eyes.' He stripped the leaves from the plant, leaving a small white fleshy root. He put the root in his mouth, chewed it vigorously, and then held the spittle there while he took the child forcibly from Mrs. Farquar. He gripped Teddy between his knees and pressed the balls of his thumbs into the swollen eyes. The child screamed and Mrs Farquar cried out in protest. But Gideon took no notice. He knelt over the writhing child, pushing back the puffy lids till chinks of eyeball showed, and then he spat hard again and again. He finally lifted Teddy gently into his mother's arms and said: 'His eyes will get better.' But Mrs Farquar was weeping with terror and could hardly thank him; it was impossible to believe that Teddy could keep his sight. In a couple of hours the swellings were gone, the eyes were inflamed and tender, but Teddy could see. Mr and Mrs Farquar thanked Gideon over and over again. They felt they could do nothing to express their gratitude. They gave Gideon presents for his wife and children, and a big increase in wages, but these things could not pay for Teddy's now completely cured eyes. Mrs Farquar said: 'Gideon, God chose you as an instrument for His goodness,' and Gideon said: 'Yes, Missus, God is very good.'

All the neighbours heard the story of Teddy's cure. Up and down the district people began to tell anecdotes, reminding each other of similar things that had happened to them. But they spoke with some exasperation, because they knew that while in the bush of Africa are waiting valuable drugs locked in barks, in simple-looking leaves and roots, it was impossible to ever get the truth of them from the natives themselves.

The story eventually reached town where a doctor challenged it. 'Nonsense,' he said, 'these things get exaggerated in the talking. We are always checking up on this kind of story and we draw a blank every time.' One morning he arrived at the homestead with one of the workers from the laboratory carrying cases of test-tubes and chemicals. The Farquars were pleased and flattered. They asked him to lunch. They told the story over and over again, and the scientist explained how humanity might benefit if this new drug could be offered for sale. When the scientist talked about the money that they could make the Farquars who were simple religious folk were rather uncomfortable. So he talked again about the benefits to humanity that could result from the sale of the drug. That pleased the Farquars. They called Gideon into their living room and explained it all to him in a language they might use when talking to a child or someone very simple of mind. 'This Baas here, is a Big Doctor from the Big City', they said 'and he has come all the way to see you.' And Mrs Farquar smiled in a kind sort of way.

Gideon seemed to look afraid, as if he didn't understand, and Mrs Farquar explained quickly that it was because of the wonderful thing he had done with Teddy's eyes that the Big Baas had come. Now at this Gideon looked reproachfully at his white employers, as if he could not believe that his old friends could so betray him. Mrs Farquar tried to explain to him how a useful medicine could be made from the root and put on sale, and how thousands of people in Africa, both black and white, could be saved from blindness. Gideon did not reply. The scientist, smiling with sceptical good humour, chipped in and explained all over again, in different words, about the making of drugs and the progress of science. Also, he offered Gideon a present.

Gideon's manner became sullen and hostile. He remarked indifferently that he could not remember the root. The Farquars began to feel annoyed. But they all realised nothing would make him give in. The magical drug wold remain where it was, unknown and useless except for the tiny scattering of Africans who had the knowledge, natives who might be digging a ditch for the municipality in a ragged shirt and a pair of patched shorts, but who were still born to healing, hereditary healers, being the nephews or sons of the old witch doctors whose ugly masks and bits of bone and all the uncouth properties of magic were the outward signs of real power and wisdom.

The Farquars might tread on that plant fifty times a day, but they would never know it.

(Abridged and simplified from *No Witchcraft for Sale* by Doris Lessing)

If you would like to know how the story ends, read on.:

They went on persuading and arguing, and Gideon continued to say he could not remember. He was rude and stubborn and didn't care that he contradicted himself and appeared stupid.

Then suddenly he lifted his head, and gave a long blank angry look at the whites, who seemed to him like a circle of yelping dogs pressing around him, and snarled: 'I will show you the root.' Then he led them in a single file on that blazing afternoon, down a path.

For two hours he walked them through the unknown bush in that melting, destroying heat. The Farquars were angry, the scientist triumphant: he felt he was being proved right again: there was no such plant.

Finally Gideon picked up with deliberate casualness, a handful of blue flowers from the bush grass, flowers that had been growing plentifully all down the paths they had come. He handed them to the scientist without even looking at him, and marched off by himself on the way home.

The scientist went away, smiling in triumph, and Gideon returned to the kitchen. But for a long time after that he sulked and spoke to Mrs Farquar like an unwilling servant. After a while the soreness between the Farquars and Gideon was forgotten, they began to joke: 'When are you going to show us the snake-root, Gideon?' they would ask. And he would laugh and say, a little uncomfortably: 'But I did show you, Missus, have you forgotton?'

Much later, as a schoolboy, Teddy would come into the kitchen and say: 'You old rascal, Gideon! Do you remember the time you tricked us all by making us walk miles all over the veld for nothing? It was so far, my father had to carry me!' Teddy was really grown-up now and had learnt to talk like a grown-up white Baas speaks to his African servant. And Gideon would double up with polite laughter. After much laughing, he would straighten himself up, wipe his old eyes and look sadly at Teddy, who was grinning mischievously at him: 'Ah, Little Yellow Head, how you have grown! Soon you will be grown up with a farm of your own ...'

Glossary

The bush :	uncleared, wild country. We use the word 'bush' in this context especially when we talk about Africa or Australia.
exasperation :	annoyance
Baas :	Afrikaan word meaning Master
sceptical :	unbelieving
to chip in :	to interrupt a conversation suddenly with an opinion
hostile :	unfriendly, showing dislike

Vocabulary

A. *Which word or words in the list mean the same or nearly the same as the first one? The first word has been used according to its meaning in the text and so your synonym must be according to the text.*

distant :	far, a long way off, aloof, arrogant, shy.
stagger :	toddle, gallop, walk, stroll, walk unsteadily.
gratitude :	generosity, thankfulness, kindness, gratification, earnestness.
sceptical :	proud, lazy, unbelieving, irritating, humorous.
uncouth :	stupid, undying, unbelieving, unnecessary, rough in manner and appearance.
file :	circle, square, line, queue, instrument to shape nails.
sullen :	gloomy, hot-tempered, ill-humoured and unsociable, laughter-loving, flippant.
triumphant :	disdainful, sly, victorious, pious, religious.

B. *The letters of these words are jumbled up. Rearrange the letters to form sensible words from the story.*

ovssiimchue :	bad but not seriously bad (especially behaviour of children) probably causing trouble or damage

ideelatbre :	on purpose, intentional
ingr :	a wide smile
eellhngca :	to call someone to compete against one especially in a fight or match
rusdapee :	try to make someone do something by arguing, reasoning, coaxing or begging
vilbeee :	consider to be true or honest
ctiirsdt :	an area of a country or state with its own local government
asgwe :	daily or weekly payment for labour or service
past :	past tense of 'spit'
ncikh :	a narrow opening or crack
lfidmnea :	red and swollen because hurt or diseased
edtacneo :	a short, interesting or amusing story about a person or event

Comprehension

A. *Complete these sentences with the correct ending.*

1. If it hadn't been for Gideon's quick action
   a. Teddy would have been completely cured.
   b. Teddy would have gone blind.
   c. Teddy would have been grateful.
   d. Mrs Farquar would have saved Teddy's eyes.
2. Gideon accepted his position as
   a. one who knew all about medicines.
   b. an important member of the household.
   c. a servant in the Farquar household.
   d. Mrs Farquar's adviser on important matters.
3. The old cook knew
   a. the properties of the medicinal root.
   b. about God and his goodness.
   c. that the tree-snake was hanging by its tail from the roof.
   d. that Teddy would not live.

4. The doctor from the city
   a. didn't really believe the story of Teddy's cure.
   b. was a jolly, kindly soul.
   c. was Teddy's constant companion.
   d. offered to help Gideon in his search.
5. The knowledge of medicinal roots and herbs was
   a. sold by Gideon and the other native Africans.
   b. studied by the scientist from the city.
   c. cherished and kept secret by the native Africans.
   d. for sale.
6. The white settlers like the Farquars
   a. were sensitive and understood how the native Africans felt about things.
   b. did not understand the deeper emotions and feelings of the native African people.
   c. had a deep respect for native African medicines.
   d. lived in busy modern cities.
7. The native Africans are often poor and look ragged but they
   a. refuse to work.
   b. have wisdom and they know the secrets of valuable medicinal herbs and roots, which grow in the bush.
   c. have large bank balances hidden away.
   d. are well fed and well looked after.

B. *Mark the true statements T, the false ones F and the ones about which the text doesn't say anything DS. Correct the false ones if you can.*

1. Gideon had his own traditions and culture which the Farqurs understood and respected greatly.
2. Teddy and the native African children did not play together as equals.
3. Teddy was very fond of Gideon.
4. The scientist was a wise and sympathetic man.
5. The scientist believed that the blue flowers were the snake-root.
6. The scientist had no respect at all for the white settlers.
7. The scientist had had all his education in Europe.
8. The hero of this story is Teddy.
9. Teddy grew up to be a Big Baas as Gideon had predicted.
10. The Farquars were cruel to their African employees.

C. *Match the answers in Box B with the questions in Box A.*

A	B
1. What did Gideon feel about the difference between his own child and Teddy?	*a. They were secretive about their medicines and seemed stubborn and unreasonable.*
2. Why did Gideon become distant and formal towards Teddy as the boy grew up?	*b. He had never believed the story of Teddy's cure and had challenged it. And now Gideon's action and behaviour, he thought, proved him right.*
3. What was it about white children that fascinated the black?	*c. He walked them through miles of bush in the melting, destroying heat and then gave them some common, worthless blue flowers.*
4. Why did Teddy touch Gideon's son's cheek and hair?	*d. He was curious because the child's skin and hair were so different from his own.*
5. Why were the white people exasperated with the natives?	*e. That it was God's will that one would grow up to be a master and the other a servant.*
6. What did Gideon do to teach the scientist and the Farquars a lesson?	*f. The scientist whom they respected greatly visited them and talked to them.*
7. Why did the scientist feel triumphant?	*g. Their yellow hair and light eyes.*
8. Why were the Farquars pleased and flattered?	*h. He accepted his position as servant and Teddy's as master as something natural in God's ordered universe and did not want to interfere with it.*

5. The Night the Policemen Came

In this story by Shashi Deshpande you read about a family of four, Amma and her three children, and the manner in which they face the policemen who enter their house at night to make a search.

The story is taken from *The Narayanpur Incident*, a book about the Quit India Movement of 1942.

For long after, even when they were grown up, Babu and Manju remembered that night. It was like a nightmare, all those huge, burly figures filling up their small, tidy house. The electricity had, as it often did, failed, and there was only a kerosene lantern on the floor to provide some light. It threw strange, wavering shadows on the walls. The policemen's shadows were grotesque and gigantic, reaching up to the ceiling, making the house seem even more crowded than it really was. There were also, adding to the illusion of a crowd in the house, the harsh sounds of the policemen's footwear on the stone floor.

'They walked in with their shoes on,' Amma complained bitterly, the one time, the only time, she spoke of it later. 'They didn't spare even the puja room and the kitchen.'

There were ugly scraping, screeching sounds as the men pulled out trunks, and loud clangs as they let the lids fall down carelessly when they had done searching inside.

There was a small black trunk in which Manju kept her treasures — coloured pictures, two old wooden dolls, a tiny silver purse and a collection of shells that Manju had gathered when they had gone the year before on a holiday to Karwar. The policemen opened this trunk too, and after going through its contents, contemptuously dropped the shells all over the floor. As they walked about, the delicate shells cracked and crunched under their feet — tiny, crackling sounds that hurt Manju more than anything else. She had been standing quietly until then, as Amma, Mohan and Babu were doing. Now, as the shells crunched into bits, she made a sudden movement and a horrified sound. And then she felt Amma's hand, which had been quietly resting on her shoulder, press down as if restraining or comforting her. Manju looked up questioningly at her. But Amma's face was stony. There was no expression on it.

And then they were gone, angry in their disappointment that they had found nothing, hateful in their anger, leaving behind them a dirty, littered home, and four persons savage with anger. And silence.

It was Amma who came out of it first. 'Come on, all of you,' she said, her voice as flat and expressionless as her face had been earlier, 'let's clear up.'

They set to work in silence. Amma, in spite of the late hour, even washed the floor as if she wanted to wipe out all traces of those hateful feet. And Mohan, who usually grumbled about Amma's 'cleanliness' helped her without a word. At last they had done, and unrolling their mattresses, they tried to get to sleep. It had been a long day — was it only yesterday that Appa had been arrested? — and they were tired. Still, Babu found himself awake. And he guessed from the restless movements that came from Mohan's bed, that Mohan couldn't sleep either.

A little later Amma called out, 'Mohan?'

'Yes, Amma?'

'Awake?'

'Yes.'

Amma came in. 'Mohan, I've been thinking. Who knew that you would bring the cyclostyling machine here today?'

'Why, Amma?'

'Well, how did the police come to know? They were very definite about it. Someone must have told them.'

Mohan whistled through his teeth. 'Of course! You're right.'

'How many people knew about it?'

'There's Bhausaheb, Mukand, Suman. Maybe Shiva, and one or two others. I don't know who else, Amma.'

'You know what this means. There's a traitor somewhere.'

There was a soft thud as if Mohan had hit something — his pillow, maybe. 'Traitors, traitors. God, always traitors. That's how we lost our country. Will we lose it again?'

(From *The Narayanpur Incident* by Shashi Deshpande)

Glossary

nightmare : a frightening dream
burly : big and strong; heavily built
wavering : moving about unsteadily
grotesque : unnaturally distorted; of unnatural, comical or frightening shape
illusion : a false belief or theory; something that creates a feeling that it is real, but is not so at all
contempt : scorn; the attitude of looking down on someone
traitor : a disloyal person, especially to ones own country

Vocabulary

A. *The word 'sound' can be used both as a noun (naming word) as well as a verb (action word).*

e.g. There were ugly, scraping, screeching *sounds* as the men pulled out trunks. *(The word 'sound' is used here as a noun.)*
As soon as the siren sounded the people ran into the air-raid shelter. *(Here 'sound' is used as a verb or action word.)*

Fill in the blanks in the sentences using the appropriate word from the box. (Remember to make the necessary changes in the word according to the tense of the verb.)

crowd	*wonder*	*question*
fire	*guess*	*face*

1. a. When the policemen ______________ Amma she answered them quite fearlessly.
   b. The officer asked Amma many ______________ which she answered fearlessly.
2. a. The people who watched were full of ______________ at the boy's courage.
   b. They ______________ what would happen to the family if Mohan was arrested.
3. a. A large ______________ had gathered outside the jail.
   b. The children ______________ round the storyteller begging him to tell them a story.
4. a. If you ______________ correctly and tell me what's in the parcel I'll give you a silver coin.
   b. I'll give you three ______________!
5. a. Amma's life was not an easy one, but she ______________ all her troubles with courage.
   b. Babu's ______________ always wears a cheerful smile.
6. a. We could hear the sound of shots being ______________ in the distance.
   b. The ______________ burnt down the railway station.

B. *Use the appropriate word from box A to fill in the blanks in the sentences in box B.*

Box A

definite
grotesque
comforted
betray
waver
restrain
provide
delicate

Box B

1. *Javed is so fond of books that if you don't ______________ him he will spend all his money on them.*
2. *The child sobbed and cried and refused to be ______________.*
3. *Appa was imprisoned, tortured and even threatened with death, but he refused to ______________ the freedom fighters.*
4. *We think Radha is arriving today, but we have no ______________ information.*
5. *Meera dressed up as a ghost. Her painted face looked quite ______________ in the blue light.*
6. *A flower is a ______________ thing; hold it carefully, or you may destroy it.*
7. *I hope they will not cut down these lovely jackfruit trees; they ______________ us not only with fruit but also with cool shade during the summer months.*
8. *You must decide soon about which job you want to take. If you ______________ you will lose them both.*

C. *Find the word or words in the text which is/are the opposite of:*

beautiful	gentle	forgot	tiny
noise	reality	later	untidy

D *Give the meaning of each of the following in one word. (Choose the word from the list in the box. You may use the dictionary to find out the meanings of words.)*

to foretell the future
to be stopped, especially by the police
to say loudly
to say again
to say under one's breath
to speak indistinctly

repeat	*mumble*
whisper	*shout*
prophesy	*arrest*

Comprehension

A. *Tick off the correct endings of the sentences according to the text.*

1. The policemen had entered the house
   a. to carry away the furniture.
   b. to search for a cyclostyling machine.
   c. to arrest the family and put them in jail.
   d. for a hot cup of coffee.
2. The kerosene lamp
   a. reached up to the ceiling.
   b. made the shadows look huge and distorted.
   c. belonged to the policemen.
   d. had gone out and left the room in darkness.
3. Manju's treasures were very precious because they
   a. cost a great deal of money.
   b. were very rare.
   c. had been given to her by a very dear friend.
   d. were her own things and she loved them.
4. The policemen did not understand
   a. English.
   b. what to do.
   c. Manju's feelings.
   d. who to talk to.
5. At the end of the policemen's visit, Amma and the children
   a. thought it was all a big joke.
   b. were so angry that they couldn't speak.
   c. grumbled loud and long.
   d. were quite calm and unruffled.

6. The policemen were angry and disappointed because
   a. the family didn't help them in any way.
   b. they couldn't leave the place and go home.
   c. they couldn't tidy up the house and clean it.
   d. they couldn't find what they had come for.
7. Amma guessed that
   a. a traitor had informed the police about the cyclostyling machine.
   b. a traitor had been arrested.
   c. traitors should be punished.
   d. traitors lost our country.
8. Even after many years had gone by and Manju and her brothers had grown up, they
   a. remembered the night of the police raid.
   b. tried to find out who the traitor was.
   c. made every effort to recover what the police had carried away.
   d. did all they could to bring peace to the unhappy land.

B. *Match the questions in Box A with the answers in Box B.*

Box A	Box B
1. What made Amma very bitter against the policemen?	a. Their disappointment that they had found nothing.
2. What happened when the policemen trampled on Manju's shells?	b. Traitors, traitors, God, always traitors. That's how we lost our country. Will we lose it again?
3. What made the house seem even more crowded than it really was?	c. They walked with their shoes on. They didn't spare even the *puja* room and the kitchen.
4. What made the policemen angry?	d. They cracked and crunched under their feet.
5. What did Mohan say when Amma told him she thought there was a traitor somewhere?	e. The policemen's shadows — grotesque and giagantic, reaching up to the ceiling.

C. *Mark the true statements T and the false ones F. Correct the false statements if you can. Write DS against those statements about which the text doesn't say anything.*

1. The policemen were careless and rough with the family's belongings.
2. Though he was tired Babu lay awake for a long time until the policemen arrived.
3. Amma knew that the police had come to arrest them.
4. Amma guessed that the police had come to know about the cyclostyling machine, because they told her what they thought.
5. The children and their mother had a frightening dream that the police had raided the house.
6. Mohan usually grumbled about his mother's insistence on cleanliness.
7. Mohan loved to whistle.
8. Amma believed that there was someone who had betrayed them to the police.
9. Babu and Manju forgot that terrible night when the police raided their house.
10. Amma spoke about the raid very often afterwards.

6. The Story of Balder

Balder's nights were troubled with fearful dreams. A shadow, a presence followed him constantly. At first he didn't know its name. But one day he heard it whispered; the name was Death. When Balder spoke to his friends about it they laughed and tried to brush aside his fears, 'Why should you be afraid? You are young, strong, healthy. There's nothing wrong with you.'

But Balder shook his head and his eyes were sad. His friends tried to persuade him to join their games and sports again; ever since these dreams had started Balder had stayed away from them. This had disappointed them terribly because Balder had been the best player of them all. Whether it was archery or riding, fencing or swimming Balder had always won every contest with ease and grace. So he was the darling of every heart, popular because he was handsome, skilled and laughter-loving. Besides he was large-hearted and generous. He could sing and dance and enliven the dullest company with his ready wit. So it was not surprising that everyone loved Balder, and when he suddenly became silent and melancholic they could not understand it. They spoke to his parents about it — to Odin his father and Frigga his mother.

Finally Odin decided to ride down to Hel, the country of the dead and meet its queen. He hoped he would be able to make a pact with her. But the queen of Hel would make no pact with him, though he was a king and wielded immense power. Powerful he may be, but as far as death was concerned, nobody could overcome that. All she told him was that Balder was destined to die and his death would not be long now. So Odin returned heavy-hearted from his mission, and told Frigga his wife how he had failed. But Frigga wouldn't take this for an answer.

'If the queen of Hel will not be reasonable, we must work to prevent death from touching Balder,' she said. She set out on a long journey. She travelled everywhere and spoke to everything, to every beast and bird, insect and reptile and begged each not to harm Balder. They gave her their word because they loved the boy and pitied the grieving mother. She spoke to air and water, wind and soil and they too gave their word. She went to the underground regions and the creatures that inhabit them swore not to harm Balder. The minerals and metals, rocks and stones all promised that they wouldn't so much as touch a hair of his head. When all the inhabitants of the many worlds had promised, Frigga began her homeward journey, confident that her son wouldn't die now, that nothing would kill him. On the way back something caught her eye, a tiny plant that grew out of a great oak tree, a pretty plant with bright green leaves and red berries. As she went hurrying past it, she remembered that she had not seen this plant before nor spoken to it. The mistletoe had not given any promise. 'But,' thought Frigga, 'what of it? It's only a tiny thing. It couldn't possibly do any harm.' She was in a great hurry to be back and to announce to everyone the good news of what she had achieved. She had no time to talk to the harmless-looking mistletoe.

Frigga arrived in her own country and when Balder's friends heard her news they were overjoyed. Balder himself began to smile again; his sadness began to recede and he returned to the games and sports and amusements that he had once taken pleasure in. His friends were delighted for they had missed him these many days.

One day they thought of a new sport. 'Let's throw things at Balder and see for ourselves how far he is immune,' someone suggested. There was general approval. They made Balder stand against a tree and hurled things at him — small things at first like pebbles and stones and then, when they found that these fell away from him without harming him, they grew bolder and threw bigger and more dangerous things like rocks and flaming torches and knives and swords and darts with poisoned heads. They flung the fangs of tigers and wolves and the claws of great birds of prey. Balder stood quite unharmed. 'He really is invulnerable,' said everyone rejoicing.

Everyone? Did I say everyone? I was wrong. For there was one person who didn't rejoice and that was Loki. Loki could not bear to see the sight of so much unalloyed happiness. Loki was wicked; mischief and trouble were Loki's life-breath. He came sidling up to Frigga, disguised as an old woman and talked to her and wrested from her the information that she had neglected to take the oath from the mistletoe. 'Why! There lies my answer!' chortled Loki to himself. He sped away to the oak tree that harboured the mistletoe. He cut the little plant and in a secret hiding place he chiselled and shaped it into an arrowhead. Then he made his way to the playground where Balder's friends were at their games. Loki looked about him stealthily until in a far corner he spotted the figure of a young man who stood alone. Recognising the figure as Hod, Balder's blind brother, Loki crept up to him. 'Hod, why do you stand alone?' asked Loki.

'Because I have no weapon and I do not know how to make one. Don't you see I am blind?'

'That's sad!' Loki murmured, his voice soft and sympathetic. 'Wouldn't you like to join the others at their game — you who are Balder's brother?'

'I would,' Hod answered, 'but I have told you I have no weapon.'

'That's sad!' Loki murmured, his voice soft and sympathetic. 'Wouldnt you like to join the others at their game — you who are Balder's brother?'

'I would,' Hod answered, 'but I have told you I have no weapon.'

'Why, that's no problem,' Loki said. 'I'll give you a weapon.'

Hod drew back, 'No, no. Your weapon might hurt Balder. I wouldn't like to take a risk.'

'Hurt Balder!' exclaimed Loki. 'Don't you know that nothing can harm Balder? Your mother has seen to that.'

Hod was silent but on his face was a wistfulness Loki did not fail to notice. 'Come on,' urged Loki. 'What are you afraid of? You mustn't stand here fretting while all the rest are having fun!'

Hod held out a trembling hand and Loki thrust the misletoe arrow into it. 'Come now. Throw this at your brother. Feel it! It's only a sprig of tender green leaves.' Hod's fingers touched it, closed on it.

'Take aim now and let it fly.'

Hod took aim and let the misletoe fly. It made its way towards Balder amid the weapons his friends were hurling at him. The misletoe pierced Balder's clothes and skin. It touched his heart. The blood spurted out and gushed forth.

The lad uttered a cry, staggered and fell, and when the frightened young men and women ran to him, they found him already dead.

They wept bitterly – and Hod, poor, blind Hod – when he learnt what his hand had done he wept the most and no one could comfort him. After a while, Hod sobbed out the story of the stranger who had thrust the mistletoe into his hand and wheedled him into using it. When they heard this Balder's friends guessed it was the doing of Loki. They clenched their fists and they swore they would find him out and punish him for Balder's death.

(retold by Shanta Rameshwar Rao)

Glossary

large-hearted :	not mean or miserly; generous
enliven :	to make more lively or cheerful.
melancholy :	sadness which extends over a long period and has no particular reason or cause
pact :	a solemn agreement.
wield :	to control the action of (A ruler wields power in his country. A religious teacher can wield enermous power in the area in which he or she works.)
mission :	the duty or purpose for which certain people are sent
recede :	to move back or away
approval :	to approve is to consider something good or right or wise. Approval is the act of approving
vulnerable :	easily harmed, hurt or attacked
invulnerable :	that which cannot be harmed, hurt or attacked
to neglect :	to give too little attention or care to; to fail to do something because of carelessness
to harbour :	to give protection and shelter – especially to someone or something undesirable.
a chisel :	a metal tool with a sharp blade used for cutting into or shaping wood, stone, etc.
to chisel :	to cut or shape with a chisel
unalloyed :	unmixed (An alloy is a mixture of several metals.)
to sidle up to someone :	to go close to someone with a stealthy sideways motion
to chortle :	to chuckle gleefully; to make the sound of laughter inside the throat
stealthy :	a movement such as a thief might make when he wants to escape notice (Stealthy comes from the word steal.)
wheedle :	to persuade by flattering and coaxing

Vocabulary

A. *Which word or words from the box would you use to describe:*

Frigga	Odin	Hod	Balder	Balder's friends
cavern	warrior	plant	thoughts	creeper/vine
Loki	heart	banyan tree		

crafty	*determined*	*envious*	*dark*
devious	*hopeful*	*clinging*	*scheming*
innocent	*grieving*	*gloomy*	*devoted*
gigantic	*invulnerable*	*evil*	*loving*
powerful	*unthinking*	*careless*	*broken-hearted*
diffident	*unspoken*	*sly*	*unsuspecting*
ill-fated	*massive*		

B. *Make new words.*

1. Form nouns from the following:

large-hearted	vulnerable
grant	decide
cheerful	describe

2. Form adjectives from the following:

gloom	generosity	miser
globe	care	melancholy

3. What verbs can you form from the following?

glory	short	life
terror	dark	rear

C. *Classify the nouns below, under the following heads:*

1. Musical instruments
2. Sports
3. Plants
4. The cosmos
5. States of mind

star	*guitar*	*outer space*	*reveries*	*thoughts*
pride	*triple*	*jump*	*neem*	*archery*
grass	*violin*	*saxophone*	*asteroid*	*cello*
imaginings	*ukelele*	*pole-vaulting*	*hurdling*	*bamboo*
swimming	*dreams*	*harmonica*	*trombone*	*fears*
nightmares	*fencing*	*planet*	*banjo*	*meteor*
flute	*solar system*	*hopes*	*comet*	*lunar-landscape*
memory	*hibiscus*	*mistletoe*	*anxiety*	*chrysanthemum*

D. *The verbs in the passage below have been substituted with the word* ***diddle.*** *Replace the* ***diddles*** *with suitable verbs.*

My mother *diddled* books. She *diddled* them from friends and *diddled* them home to *diddle* out to us, every evening by the light of the hurricane lamp. That was why she *diddled* those lamps so industriously every evening, *diddling* the wicks, *diddling* the glass until it *diddled* clean of every spot and stain.

E. *Fill in the blanks with the opposites of the words in italics from the list in the box.*

diffident	*weak*
cautious	*succeeded*
miserly	*lazy*
clumsy	*questions*
life	*shouts*
mean	*brilliant*

1. Though Frigga ____________ in persuading many creatures not to harm Balder she *failed* to prevent his death.
2. Though he is rich and has a thriving business he is quite ____________ while his neighbour who is not wealthy is far two *extravagant.*
3. *Death* and ____________ they say are twins, both born at the same time.
4. The bear is rather a ____________ beast, whereas the tiger's movements are extraordinarily *graceful.*
5. Although he was a rather *dull* student at school when he was young, he grew up to be a ____________ mathematician.
6. Sometimes she *whispers* so softly I can't hear her; at other times she ____________ so loud that I feel my ear-drums will burst.
7. His *answers* never match the ____________ .
8. The mother is as ____________ as the daughter is *hardworking.*
9. To be *generous* and forgiving is far, far better than to be ____________ and vindictive.
10. He pretends to be *bold* and daring, while he's really quite ____________ and doesn't like to take any risks.

11. There's always the danger of the *powerful* nations threatening the ______________ ones.
12. Though I used to be *confident* and sure of myself once, today I feel very ______________ about being able to speak in public.

Comprehension

A. *Tick off the correct endings to these sentences:*

1. What really troubled Balder was the fear of
   a. Loki.
   b. death.
   c. nightmares and bad dreams.
   d. dreams of death.
2. Not only were his friends concerned about Balder's fears but also
   a. Loki.
   b. his own inner thoughts.
   c. his parents.
   d. his worst enemies.
3. Balder had always been
   a. a good sportsman.
   b. rather scared of shadows.
   c. arrogant and conceited.
   d. jealous of his brother Hod.
4. The Queen of Hel
   a. wouldn't give Odin any promise.
   b. promised Odin that she would protect Balder.
   c. hated Balder and so wanted to kill him.
   d. was a friend of Loki the wicked one.
5. People enjoyed Balder's company because
   a. he was informal and easy-going.
   b. he was always making fun of people and teasing them.
   c. he played games.
   d. of his many good qualities.
6. Frigga made every creature
   a. give its word that it would harm Balder.
   b. promise to harm the mistletoe.
   c. except one swear not to harm Balder.
   d. swear not to die.

7. It was for her son that Frigga
   a. talked to Loki.
   b. undertook the long journey.
   c. obeyed the mistletoe.
   d. asked his friends to hurl stones at him.
8. Balder's friends wanted to
   a. try their skill at throwing stones and darts and torches.
   b. kill Frigga for betraying them.
   c. test the strength of the mistletoe.
   d. play a game and test the truth of Frigga's words.
9. Balder's death was brought about by
   a. the hissing venomous snake.
   b. his unsuspecting brother.
   c. his own dreams and nightmares.
   d. the Queen of Hel.
10. Balder's friends could not revive him because
    a. death is final and there's no return from death.
    b. they didn't try hard enough.
    c. Loki wouldn't let them.
    d. he wanted to die.

B. *Mark the true statements T, the false ones F. Mark the ones about which the text does not say anything DS. Correct the false statements.*

1. Odin went to the country of the dead in order to meet Frigga.
2. Balder's mother was able to persuade everything not to harm him.
3. Balder was frightened of nothing — not even death.
4. Balder was young, strong and healthy.
5. It was the mistletoe that killed Balder.
6. Frigga overlooked the mistletoe which grew inside a cave.
7. The oak tree sheltered the mistletoe.
8. Odin didn't care about Balder.
9. Odin didn't believe the Queen of Hel.
10. The Queen of Hel knew that Balder had decided to die.
11. Balder would have been immortal if Odin had taken precautions.
12. Frigga and Odin loved Hod better than Balder.
13. Balder was handsome but he was rather bald.

14. Hod pretended to be blind.
15. Frigga was just a little careless.

C. *Find the lines in the story that have the same meaning as the lines below:*

1. Whatever games or sports he took part in, Balder had never known defeat; besides he played (games) effortlessly and his movements were beautiful.
2. He was certainly not selfish, mean or miserly.
3. He grew depressed and morose and he stopped talking and laughing.
4. Though he had great strength, influence and control over people, when it came to the question of death, he realised that he could do nothing against it.
5. It was pre-determined that Balder would die soon.
6. Everybody felt that this was a good thing to do.
7. They were happy to see that he was strong and that nothing could hurt him.
8. By using many tricks and devices he forced out from her the fact that she had not troubled to make the mistletoe give its word (not to harm Balder).
9. The mistletoe had its home inside the oak tree.
10. Hod told how a person he had never seen before had put the mistletoe into his hand and coaxed and persuaded him to use it.

7. Not Just Oranges

In a city, never mind what it was called, there lived a small girl of about five. The little girl had a mother and no one else. They lived together, the two of them, not well, not badly, but a life of some hardship. The mother was a charwoman — the income was meagre, every kopek had to be saved. But the girl was fed, dressed and had shoes on her feet. And the mother brought a lot of different goodies from the hospital — sometimes candy, sometimes apples. The patients often gave her treats. Especially when they were being discharged. They were too happy to bother about carrying things back and so gave them away to the little girl's mother. They even gave away oranges. But patients who had oranges to give away were few and far between, perhaps they went to other hospitals. Or perhaps they were discharged less frequently ...

Anyhow this has nothing to do with oranges ...

'We'll still live,' the mother joked.

'We'll still live,' the girl agreed.

But frankly speaking, the girl badly needed a wonderful blue ball, which she and her mother had seen in a toy shop. She felt she simply must acquire it for a truly happy life.

If you remember what it was like when you were five, you will understand what happened when the blue ball finally turned up in the girl's hands.

When the ball bounced, the little girl bounced and even the mother gave a little bounce. Because happiness makes everyone bounce a bit.

But the happiness was short-lived.

One day when the little girl was playing in the courtyard, the ball bounced so fast and so high that it flew into the window of the neighbours, the Malachovs'. And they had a vase with flowers on the windowsill. The ball went straight into the case and threw it down, and the vase shattered into pieces.

And the vase was awfully expensive and made of crystal.

The old lady stormed out into the courtyard, put her hands on her hips and announced that they had been robbed. She complained so long and so loud that other neighbours began to collect and the little girl hid from fright in a shed.

Only when the old man came out did the old lady shut up.

Soon after that, the little girl's mother returned from work. People told her everything and she sighed and began to cry. The little girl saw her weeping mother through a slit in the door, ran to her, hugged her, and also crying, began to say how sorry she was.

'My foolish one ...' was all the mother said before she took her daughter's hand. So they went hand in hand to the Malachovs'.

The old lady gave her such a look that the little girl cringed. 'There they are,' said the old lady rudely and reached out to pull the little girl's plait. But she caught the old man's stern glance and drew her hands away, growing quiet.

'We'll pay for it,' said the little girl's mother, biting her lip. 'Please don't worry, we'll definitely pay ...'

'We'll pay,' the daughter said.

'Don't I know you'll pay ...' the old man jibed, '... Just look at you!'

On the floor, next to the window, under the dully shining splinters of crystal, lay the crumpled flowers in a sparkling pool. The old lady had purposely not cleaned it up.

'Are they dead?' asked the girl.

The old man gave a start.

'Look who can pay!' he suddenly shouted, and beat his fist angrily on the table.

'What windfall do you hope for to pay from? I'm asking you! Speak up!'

'Why, but why not ...?' The little girl's mother grew confused.

She tried to say something more, but old Malachov waved her aside and yelled:

'Enough, get going!'

Thus ended the visit of the offenders.

No one, naturally, remembered the ball in all the hullaballoo. Except of course the little girl.

A half hour later, the old lady Malachova herself appeared at the doorstep of the culprits. Awkwardly, with both hands, as if it were a water-melon, she held the ill-fated ball against her stomach.

'Is she asleep?' she asked softly, nodding towards the bed where the little girl lay curled up like a bundle.

'Who knows,' sighed the mother. 'Maybe she is. She cried her heart out ...' The old lady angrily held out the ball.

'Here ... And I don't want your money, don't ...!' She pressed her lips looking hurt.

The girl's mother began to fuss around, quickly found two huge, luscious oranges and forcibly thrust an orange into each of Malachova's hands.

Malachova was stunned and taken aback. Out of confusion and embarrassment, she began to smell the oranges one by one. But she suddenly stopped and, not saying a word, walked up to the sleeping little girl. She stood there, took a deep breath, and carefully put the oranges right next to the girl's pillow.

(by Isai Tobolsky,
translated from Russian
by Kamakshi Balasubramanian)

Glossary

charwoman : a woman who is employed to clean homes or public buildings

meagre : small in quantity

kopek : a Russian coin: one-hundredth part of a rouble (rather like a paisa)

goodies : something good to eat

discharged : sent away or released

frank : open and direct; making no pretences

windfall : When a wind blows some ripe fruit off a tree unexpectedly, you have a *windfall*. Something of value which you receive unexpectedly is a *windfall*.

offend : hurt someone's feelings; make someone angry or disgusted

culprit : a guilty person; a person accused of an offence

ill-fated : unlucky

embarrassment : awkwardness; shyness; self-consciousness

Vocabulary

A. *'Ill-fated' is a hyphenated, compound word. It is made by joining two words: ill and fated. The words are joined together with a hyphen (s small dash).*
Make as many sensible hyphenated words as you can with the words in the two boxes below.

evil-	*curly-*	*well-*	*blue-*
white-	*dark-*	*large-*	*warm-*
stout-	*gentle-*	*strong-*	*brown-*
cruel-	*brave-*	*soft-*	*ill-*
long-	*kind-*	*black-*	*white-*

-haired
-hearted
-eyed
-brought up

B. *Fill in the blanks in the sentences below with the correct form of the word.*

1. as a noun — *storm*
   as an adjective — *stormy*
   as an adverb — *stormily*
   as a verb — *to storm; stormed; storming; etc.*
   a. It's ________ weather: a fierce wind is blowing and the rain is pouring.
   b. When his mother refused to buy him the toy, the child ________ and screamed. He's terribly spoilt.
   c. The ship was caught in a ________ at sea, and was nearly wrecked.
   d. She wept ________, her sobs catching in her throat and her tears gushing out of her swollen eyes.
2. as a noun — *sparkle*
   as a verb — *to sparkle; sparkled; sparkling ; etc.*
   as an adjective — *sparkling*
   a. The dewdrops glinted and ________ in the morning sunshine.
   b. As we stood looking on, the ________ waters of the fountain began to gush out.
   c. There was hidden laughter in her voice and a ________ of mischief in her eyes.
3. as a noun — *frequency*
   as a verb — *to frequent; frequents; etc.*

as an adverb — *frequently*
as an adjective — *frequent*

a. He's a ________ visitor around here: we know him well.
b. The ________ with which the attacks of fever occur shows that we must take you to the hospital and find out what's wrong.
c. They speak of you very ________ , and with great affection.
d. We noticed that the man in the blue suit ________ the library, and we concluded that he is very fond of reading.

C. *Complete this crossword puzzle with the help of the clues on the next page.*

Across

4 long poles, usually made of wood, used to propel boats
5 copy or mimic someone
9 send away; release
10 liquid which flows from the eyes when we weep
11 A long, thin opening
12 Male child of parent
13 costly; expensive

Down

1 A very clear and transparent kind of glass
2 This is how some people address their mother
3 Personal pronoun, third person, masculine gender
4 command
6 Maybe
7 Break into many places
8 cause
11 sorrowful

Comprehension

A. *Choose the correct ending for each of these sentences :*

1. We understand from the story that the little girl's mother was employed in a
   a. railway station.
   b. municipal office.
   c. primary school.
   d. hospital.
2. The little girl's mother
   a. earned a high salary.
   b. was so poor that she was quite desperate.
   c. was neither rich nor very poor.
   d. was fat because she overate.
3. Though the income was meagre and every kopek had to be saved, the little girl
   a. agreed with what her mother said.
   b. played in the house all day.
   c. was cared for and very well looked after.
   d. was offended because she couldn't have the blue ball.
4. For both the little girl and her mother the oranges were
   a. unripe and sour.
   b. expensive and rare.
   c. common and easily available.
   d. hard-hearted and cruel.

5. The little girl's mother, though poor,
   a. was frightened of the old lady, Malachova.
   b. wanted to pay for the vase.
   c. disliked Malachova.
   d. scolded her daughter.

6. Neither the mother nor the daughter had
   a. understood about
   b. foreseen
   c. experienced
   d. spoken about

   the trouble the blue ball would cause.

7. The author has tried to tell us that the old lady Malachova was so attached to her expensive vase that she never
   a. spoke to anyone about it.
   b. did not understand the little girl or her feelings.
   c. wanted the girl's mother to pay for it.
   d. worried greatly about what would happen.

8. There was an accident when the ball
   a. was sold.
   b. hit the crystal vase and knocked it down.
   c. was returned.
   d. was shattered.

9. The girl and her mother were
   a. sent home by the family upstairs.
   b. taken to task by Malachova and the old man.
   c. punished by their neighbours.
   d. angered by what happened.

10. The little girl's mother gave Malachova the precious and rare oranges
    a. gladly and without a murmur.
    b. with a heavy heart.
    c. grudgingly.
    d. with tears in her eyes.

B. *Match the part of the sentence in Box A with the correct part in Box B, according to the text.*

Box A	Box B
1. *There are*	a. *salary was small.*
2. *The characters are*	b. *belonged to Malachova.*
3. *The mother's*	c. *was a happy child.*
4. *Life*	d. *the little girl, her mother, the old man and Malachova.*
5. *Inspite of this the mother and daughter*	e. *shouted and complained to all the neighbours.*
6. *The little one*	f. *a big fuss about the broken vase.*
7. *Trouble began*	g. *the little girl's house.*
8. *The vase*	h. *four main characters in the story.*
9. *It was*	i. *was certainly not easy for the poor woman.*
10. *Malachova made*	j. *made of crystal and was very very expensive.*
11. *She*	k. *loved each other dearly and were very happy together.*
12. *Later she visited*	l. *when the girl accidentally broke a vase.*

C. *Mark T against the statements which are true, F against the ones that are false, and DS against those about which the text doesn't say anything.*

1. The writer doesn't tell us the name of the city where this incident took place.
2. The city where the incident took place was in Italy.
3. The patients who gave away the oranges were very poor.
4. Sometimes the patients gave the woman nice things to eat which she brought home for her daughter.
5. Patients who gave away oranges were not many.
6. Malachova deliberately left the mess on the floor.

7. If the old man had not given Malachova a stern look she would have pulled the little girl's plaits.
8. When Malachova brought the ball to the little girl's house her mother was fast asleep.
9. Malachova and the little girl became good friends after this little incident.
10. The little girl promised never to break vases again.

8. A Different Kind of Learning

Jade Snow Wong's family had come to the United States of America from Canton, China, in the opening decade of this century and settled there among other Chinese immigrants.

Jade's family had a readymade garments factory. When she passed out of school and junior college, she went to Mills College to continue her education. At first her parents were not happy at all about her going to college, because they felt college education was not necessary for girls. But though they raised many objections they finally agreed to let her enter Mills. The first few weeks at Mills were very disturbing for Jade Snow Wong.

Till then she had had her education through the traditional Chinese method. Chinese students were given information by their teachers and made to learn it exactly as it had been given. The teachers lectured and the students took down notes. They were also given specific assignments to do. Everything was done in an orderly manner; the questions asked were expected questions and the answers given were expected answers. The students learnt their lessons by heart and developed a very good memory. It was in its way a method that had been perfected.

What was disturbing in the first weeks at Mills was that her lifelong perfected system of learning failed her. At the end of several weeks, she had only a handful of lecture notes. The instructor of the labour course, a brilliant and direct man, taught by encouraging questions. But at the end of every never-dull class period, Jade Snow did not have one lecture note.

How was she going to study without notes? Accustomed to specific assignments in an orderly fashion, and habitually thorough, she became concerned by the vagueness of these subjects which defeated her ability to memorize — an ability carefully perfected by her Chinese studies and which had heretofore always worked.

Impressed by the informality and approachability of her professors, she gathered her courage to speak to her labour instructor. 'I have a problem in not being able to take any lecture notes from you. At junior college, we were given definite outlines to follow and study for examinations.'

Her instructor seemed amused. 'Why do you think that you learn only from lecture notes?'

Jade Snow had no answer to this unexpected question.

He continued, 'Here we want to know each one individually. Instead of reading a set of prepared notes, I study my students' minds and ideas. By the conversational method, I try to develop their minds, not give you sets of facts. Don't you know that you can always go to the library to look up facts?'

Jade Snow could not immediately grasp this new concept of individual training. She had never thought of the purpose of academic training as being anything else than that of disseminating superior information.

All she could say in defence was, 'But I learned a lot from junior college.'

The instructor came back neatly, 'Sure, you learned a lot. But now I am trying to teach you to think!'

Jade Snow, at a complete loss, mumbled a 'Thank you' and trailed off in a state of mental indigestion.

The first midterm gave ample exercise in how to think. Jade Snow arrived at class in a fog of memorized dates, names, and places, and found that one essay question comprised the entire midterm. It was: 'You are (choose one) a Palestinian potter; an Anatolian farmer; an Athenian shoe-maker; a Carthaginian clerk; a Roman cook; a West-Saxon weaver; an Italian goldsmith. You are transferred to Oakland in 1940, and try to get a job in your trade. What problems do you face?'

A buzz of excitement went around the astounded class. Incredulous, confused, Jade Snow reread the question and floundered miserably to find a passably imaginative answer. After spending half an hour figuring what trade to select, she chose the Palestinian potter simply because it was the first one listed, but she didn't know a thing about pottery, let alone Palestinian pottery. In the ensuing hour, her heretofore unshaken faith in the effectiveness of the Chinese study method collapsed completely.

Gradually, through successive examinations and successive classroom discussions, she learned the true meaning of her instructor's remarks, and at the end of a year's study she found that from slow beginnings she was learning to analyse and to express more readily in English what she thought. She found that her curious mind was being disciplined to work quickly and to find relationships between problems.

(from *Fifth Chinese Daughter* by Jade Snow Wong)

Glossary

lifelong perfected system of learning: a method of learning which she had made perfect over the years of her life

brilliant: brightly shining. Jade's instructor was a brilliant man whose classes were never dull. 'Brilliant', here, means extraordinarily intelligent.

heretofore : Jade's ability to memorize which had *heretofore* always helped her to get through her exams, now failed her. *Heretofore* means *until now*.

informality : A formal person is very particular about correct social behaviour and customs, an informal person is not.

concept : an idea, thought or opinion

disseminate : spread (We use the word disseminate when we are talking about ideas or seeds.)

mumble : speak indistinctly, without opening the mouth fully

incredulous : unbelieving

evaluate : comes from the word *value* and means *measure the value of*.

floundered : To flounder is to struggle blindly, to blunder.

Vocabulary

A. *Match the prefixes in Box A with the words in Box B. Some words can take more than one prefix.*

Box A

un-	*im-*	*in-*
dis-		*re-*

Box B

agree	*accurate*	*armament*
sanity	*approachable*	*reliable*
reasonable	*fill*	*write*
expected	*kind*	*tell*
advisable	*sure*	*movable*
polite	*wise*	*unite*
appear	*balance*	*advantage*
adequate	*mobile*	*intelligent*
perfect	*ability*	

B. *Which of the three in brackets is the correct word/phrase?*

1. For many generations the Chinese had practised their system of learning until it had become (useful, difficult, perfect).
2. The professor (told, encouraged, forbade) the students to ask questions.
3. The professor told Jade Snow Wong that he wanted to make his students (think for themselves, honest and trustworthy, get through their examinations).

4. Jade Snow Wong had always thought that teachers and professors were there to give their students (information, work, truth).
5. The professor reminded Miss Wong that she could always go to a (school, college, library) for information.

C. *What are these people called?*

The people of:

Athens	Denmark
Greece	Sweden
Carthage	Norway
Anatolia	Saudi Arabia
Rome	Iraq
Italy	Iran
Palestine	Nigeria
China	Korea
Japan	Indonesia
France	Pakistan

D. *Which words in the text mean the following?*

1. struck with amazement and wonder
2. spoke indistinctly
3. up to this time
4. very intelligent
5. following or coming afterwards
6. struggled helplessly in confusion
7. to determine the value of
8. following in uninterrupted order
9. unbelieving
10. a person who enters another country in order to settle in it as its citizen

E. *The suffix '-ize' is sometimes used to change a noun or an adjective into a verb.*

e.g. memory – memorize
local – localise

Add '-ize' to the nouns/adjectives below and change them into verbs. Sometimes you will need to make a change in the word before adding '-ize'

American	regular
computer	democracy
television	penalty
memory	material
terror	visual

Eight of the '-ize' words you have made can be used to fill in the blanks in the sentences below. Fill them in and complete the sentences.
(Use the appropriate form of the verb.)

1. Everything here is in disorder. There are no rules and regulations, so no one knows what to do. Unless we ______________ the system there will be no efficiency.
2. If you destroy railway property you will be ______________ . The penalty might be a fine or even imprisonment.
3. The play we are putting up on Saturday is going to be ______________ so that many people can see it on their TV.
4. They've lived in the United States for so long that they have become almost completely ______________ . They speak American English, they eat American food; they dress American-style and they sing American songs.
5. At first there was only the smell of perfume; then we heard the rustle of silk and the clink of jewellery. It was twenty minutes before the dancer ______________ on the stage.
6. In the old days children were made to ______________ their multiplication tables and to repeat them every evening.
7. The bandits had their hideout among the hills from where they swooped down on the villages, looting and robbing and ______________ the helpless villagers.
8. They do not write out bills by hand any more. They use computers to do the job. They have ______________ the whole system.

Comprehension

A. *Choose the correct ending for the sentences.*

1. We are not sure exactly when Jade Snow Wong's family first came to America — but it was sometime between:
   a. 1810 and 1910.
   b. 1983 and 1987.
   c. 1857 and 1957.
   d. 1900 and 1910.

2. They were
   a. not the only Chinese who had come to America from China.
   b. the only Chinese to come to America.
   c. settlers from the United States.
   d. welcomed warmly by the native Americans.
3. When Jade joined Mills College she found that her professors were
   a. unsympathetic.
   b. very willing to discuss her difficulties with her.
   c. formal and distant.
   d. arrogant and difficult to talk.
4. Jade had always thought that being educated in school or college meant
   a. getting a good job.
   b. collecting information which the professors gave out.
   c. spending money.
   d. learning all about Palestinian pottery.
5. She decided to write an essay on the Palestinian potter because
   a. that was the portion she had studied.
   b. she didn't care whether she passed or failed.
   c. her instructor had told her to choose that essay.
   d. it was the first in the list.

B. *Each of the boxes in Column A starts with the words Heretofore Jade and each of the boxes in Column B starts with the words but now she. Complete each sentence in Column A with the correct ending chosen from Column B.*

Column A	Column B
had been used to taking down notes from the professors' lectures	*had to make her own judgements and analyses of what she had found out.*
had been used to learning her lessons by heart	*felt as if her mind had taken in too many ideas and could not digest them.*
had memorized all her dates for the mid-term exam	*was disturbed and worried.*

had looked forward to join Mills College	*was expected to find answers and information on her own.*
had hoped all her questions would be answered by her instructor.	*was faced with an entirely different sort of question paper.*

C. *The answers for these questions are given in the boxes below. Match the answers with the questions.*

1. What did Jade Snow Wong like about her professors at Mills?
2. What did her instructor tell her?
3. What troubled Jade when she first joined Mills?
4. Why did Jade lose her faith in the effectiveness of the Chinese method of study?
5. What happened during the exam?
6. What question was Jade given to answer for the mid-term exam?

a. The method of teaching and learning here was very different from what she had been used to in junior college.

b. At Mills the students were not given notes to memorize but were encouraged to discuss their own ideas. They were taught to think for themselves.

c. She tried to write a good imaginative essay but failed.

d. They were easy to talk to, friendly and informal.

e. Jade had to imagine that she was transferred from a past age into the twentieth century.

f. When she went into the examination hall Jade found that her carefully memorized dates and names and places did not help her at all. The Chinese method of study by which students learnt their lessons by heart failed her.

9. The Election (1933)

The story below is about Germany under Adolf Hitler. A ruthless dictator, Hitler blamed Germany's defeat in World War I (1914-18) on 'enemies' inside the country — especially the Jews whom he hated. He banned all political parties except his own Nazi party. He declared that the Germans were a superior race and started a campaign to persecute and destroy the Jews. Many Jews fled the country but many were put into concentration camps where people lived in great enclosures under dreadful conditions and were starved, tortured and killed. Hitler employed his secret police, the Gestapo, to help him. He organised young people — even children — into bands to terrorise everyone. He built up Germany's military power and marched his armies into country after country in Europe until he was finally defeated in 1945 by the Allies (USSR, England, France and USA)

In January 1933 Adolf Hitler became Chancellor of the German Reich; in February the Parliament building burned; in March there were elections; in April actions against Jews began; in May the unions were dissolved; in June the political parties started dissolving on their own; in July it became illegal to found new parties; in August, holiday time, things were quieter; in September the Nazi Party 'Convention of Victory' was celebrated in Nuremberg; in October Germany left the League of Nations — and now, in November, there were more elections.

Mother was looking out of the window. 'Hmmm,' she said, 'foggy out. And cool, too.' She took my thick overcoat out of the cupboard and put a woollen scarf around my neck. I had to put on my warm cap as well.

Mother, too, wore her warmest clothes.

Then we went off to the school where the votes were to be cast.

Flags and banners lined the way to the school. Black, white, and red flags alternated with swastika flags. The banners read:

WITH ADOLF HITLER FOR PEACE!
GERMANY DEMANDS EQUALITY!

Posters showed Chancellor Adolf Hitler beside President Field Marshal von Hindenburg.

In the square, cars stood ready to drive the old and the infirm to the elections. The drivers were sitting on the running boards, playing cards.

Many people were walking towards the school. The whole town seemed to be on the move.

Father and Mother often had to exchange greetings with people they knew. Mostly it was just a 'Good morning,' but sometimes Father raised his right hand and shouted a 'Heil Hitler!' across the street. Mother merely nodded, but she, too, said, 'Heil Hitler!'

At the school innumerable signs and arrows pointed to the gymnasium. If someone hesitated, an S.A. man or a Hitler Youth immediately showed him the right way. Heinz stood in front of the entrance to the gymnasium; he was distributing sheets of paper, pressing a leaflet into the hand of each voter. He did his work conscientiously; whenever several voters approached at the same time, Heinz barred their way until he had dealt with them all.

Because Heinz was wearing a brown shirt, Mother didn't recognize him until he pressed a leaflet upon her. 'What are you doing here?' she asked, taken aback.

'I'm one of them now,' Heinz told her proudly.

Mother didn't understand. 'Of whom?' she asked.

Heinz pointed to his brown shirt, clicked his heels together, pressed his stack of leaflets against his stomach with his left hand, and placed his right hand flat against the seam of his trousers. He explained, 'Of the German Jungvolk, which is part of the Hitler Youth.'

'Is that so!' Mother said. 'And how old are you?'

'I'm ten already.'

'Well, well. Take care you don't catch cold in that thin shirt.'

Father was reading the leaflet.

'Heinz!' a shout rang across the playground. 'Heinz!'

Heinz made a quick turn towards the caller, a man in a brown uniform at the wheel of a large open car. 'Here!' he shouted. The man called again: 'Come with me!'

'Yes sir! Coming!' Heinz turned back to us. 'Please excuse me, but I must help my father bring in voters.' And he again clicked his heels together. Pointing to me with his chin, he said, 'He should become a Pimpf.'

As Heinz ran to the car and swung himself onto the seat beside his father, Father followed him with his eyes.

The car started off with a jerk, left the playground, and headed towards the suburb.

We entered the gymnasium. An attendant met us and directed me to sit on a bench by the entrance next to other children. We had to stay there until our parents had cast their votes.

Father and Mother joined the line for ballots and envelopes.

Each voter received two bits of paper, one white and one green.

'What's the good of this?' one man remonstrated. He held up the white ballot. 'You can only make an X-mark for Hitler here!' He spoke in a loud voice.

At once all talk stopped; not a sound could be heard; everyone looked at the man.

I recognized him. He was Günther's father.

'And if I don't want to vote for Hitler?' he now asked.

The attendant closed the door to the gymnasium. With a few steps he hurried over to Günther's father.

But Günther's father wouldn't let himself be interrupted. 'And this?' he shouted. In a loud voice he began to read from the green ballot:

'Do you, German man, and you, German woman, endorse the policies carried out by your government, and are you willing to affirm this government as representing your wishes and to solemnly pledge it your support?'

Before Günther's father could read more, the attendant had gripped him by the arm.

Silently, all of us in the gymnasium watched as Günther's father calmly demanded, 'Kindly let go of my arm.'

'Keep quiet!' warned the attendant. 'You are disrupting an election and influencing voters.'

Günther's father held out the two ballots to the attendant.

'Election?' He laughed. 'Kindly show me where one can choose on these chits of paper?'

The attendant did not answer.

Slowly, very slowly, Günther's father tore the ballots to shreds in full view of all those present. The shreds fluttered to the floor. Then he allowed the attendant to lead him from the gymnasium.

For a while it was uncannily quiet in the room. But after the attendant had returned alone and opened both wings of the door, everything went on as if nothing had happened. The voters disappeared into the wooden booths, and after a while they reappeared and threw their envelopes into the available ballot boxes.

(from *I was there* by Hans Peter Ritcher, translated by Edite Kroll)

Glossary

chancellor :	the Chief Minister in some European countries like the Federal Republic of Germany
Reich :	the German Empire
Jews :	an ancient group of people who lived in Palestine from the 6th century B.C. to the first century A.D. Some members of the Jewish community still live in Israel and others in various countries throughout the world. Jews follow the Judaic religion and worship Jehovah.
League of Nations :	an international organisation set up after the First World War to promote international co-operation, peace and security
Pimpf :	member of the Hitler Youth Party
Jungvolk :	young people. The youth organization of Adolf Hitler's Nazi party.
Heil Hitler :	the greeting used by the Nazi party. It was compulsory for all Germans to use this greeting when Hitler was in power.
S.A. man :	storm trooper, World War II German soldier
running boards :	one of the steps running along each side of an old car

Vocabulary

A. *Choose the right word from the box and fill in the blanks in the sentences below.*

founded	*reinstated*
rehabilitated	*endorsed*
dissolved	*cast*

1. At the end of its term, the parliament is ____________.
2. Bearer cheques need to be ____________.
2. Many educational institutions were ____________ by Raja Rammohan Roy.

4. Employees who are dismissed can be ______________.
5. Refugees who have lost all their belongings, their homes and jobs need to be ______________.
6. Votes are ______________ during an election.

B. *Tick off the most appropriate of the three meanings:*

1. to alternate
   a. to change repeatedly in turn
   b. give a choice between two options
   c. to succeed each other by turns
2. conscientious
   a. consciousness
   b. being obedient to the laws of the inner voice that tells one what is right and what is wrong
   c. very careful
3. endorse
   a. to sign away one's property to another
   b. to sign one's name on a cheque as payee in order to obtain the cash or credit represented on its face
   c. to express support of a political candidate publicly
4. disrupt
   a. to create disorder
   b. to break apart forcibly
   c. to interrupt
5. shreds
   a. to cut or tear into narrow strips
   b. narrow strips cut off neatly
   c. narrow strips torn off
6. infirm
   a. of poor quality
   b. weak in mind, will or character
   c. feeble, weak
   d. not solid or secure
7. to found is
   a. to look for
   b. to find
   c. to establish for the first time
   d. to discover

C. *By adding 'il-' at the beginning of the word 'legal' you make its opposite – 'illegal'. Other words which you can similarly change into their opposites by using 'il-' are:*

legible, legitimate, literate and logical

D. *Finding out the meaning through the root word.*

innumerable: This word has a smaller Latin word 'numer' as its root. If you find the root word, it often helps you to understand other words also derived from the same root. 'Numer' means number. So innumerable means numberless or uncountable.

Without referring to the dictionary, work out the meanings of the underlined words from the context.
(The root word is 'numer' for all of them.)

1. 'Listen' said the Great God, 'listen while I tell you the names of all things in creation.' And he went on to enumerate the names of all the hills and mountains and plains, the rivers and oceans ... and there was no end to them.
2. There's psychology which is the study of the mind; and there's physiology which is the study of the physique or body. There's palaeontology and archaeology and there's numerology! Which would you like to study?
3. The number plate on a car usually has numerals following letters.
4. Children learn to numerate from 1 to 100 when they are about six years old.
5. What is the numerator in a fraction?
6. You could put it down in alphabetical order of course or you could use the numerical order.

E. *Self-determination is a word used in civics and political science. It refers to the right of a people to decide for themselves the sort of government they wish to have.*
Some other words in the same field are:

dictator	electorate	legislature
populist	franchise	autonomy
popular	totalitarian	

Fill in the blanks in the sentences below with the appropriate word.

1. At election time it is the duty of every citizen in a democracy to exercise his ______________ or his right to vote.
2. This political leader hopes to get the votes of the masses by making them promises of higher wages, houses, telephones, schools and colleges. He uses these ______________ methods for his own ends.
3. A government voted into power by the people is called a ______________ government.
4. She was too independent in her views to be able to live in a ______________ state, where the government exercises control over all aspects of life.
5. I think that in any democracy, it is essential to educate the ______________ so that they understand their responsibility as citizens.
6. The head of the institution was quite a ______________ for he held absolute and unquestioned power in his hands and used it oppressively.

Comprehension

A. *Tick off the correct answer.*

1. Which sentence shows that the mother of the story-teller was afraid the boy might catch a cold?
   a. And now in November there were more elections.
   b. Mother was looking out of the window.
   c. She took my thick overcoat out of the cupboard and put a woollen scarf around my neck. I had to put on my warm cap as well.
   d. Then we went off to the school where the votes were to be cast.

2. Günther's father's actions show that
   a. he was hungry, and wanted his dinner more than anything else.
   b. he valued the fundamental right of people to choose their form of Government.
   c. he was an ill-mannered and foolish man.
   d. he was bent on disrupting the election and influencing the voters.

3. The story shows that the elections were
   a. noisy and disorderly.
   b. only a farce because there was no alternative to Hitler.
   c. fair and just.
   d. conducted by children by secret ballot!
4. When the story-teller's mother saw Heinz in his uniform distributing leaflets she was
   a. proud and happy.
   b. indifferent and couldn't care less.
   c. unhappy that children were used for political purposes.
   d. glad that children were learning to help in the elections.
5. Gunther's father tore the ballot paper to shreds because
   a. he disliked elections, and didn't care to vote.
   b. he felt he had no real choice, and so the election was meaningless.
   c. he was a political leader and wanted to gain power.
   c. he didn't care about his country.
6. We know that the Jungvolk, the Hitler youth movement, used children for their political activities because
   a. ten-year old Heinz distributed sheets of paper and leaflets during the election.
   b. the story-teller was directed by an attendant to sit on a bench by the entrance next to other children.
   c. both Heinz and the story-teller were children.
   d. Gunther's father tore the ballot paper to shreds.
7. Hitler was a dictator for he
   a. taught spelling and dictation.
   b. made silly mistakes.
   c. was a patriot and wanted to glorify his country.
   d. allowed no one to oppose him in whatever he did.
8. Hitler's concentration camps
   a. were held to teach German students concentration.
   b. were enclosures where large numbers of people were kept and tortured, starved and killed.
   c. were places where young Germans were given military training.
   d. were places where fruit, vegetables, etc. were cultivated during the war.

B. *Mark the statements which are true T, the ones which are false F and mark DS against the ones about which the text does not say anything. Correct the false ones if you can.*

1. The story-teller's mother knew Heinz.
2. Heinz was a grown-up man.
3. The story-teller was in uniform like Heinz.
4. Children were sent in to cast their votes along with their parents.
5. The story-teller knew Günther's father.
6. Günther's father went in to vote but in the end didn't vote at all.
7. All the people voted for the government.
8. According to Günther's father the election was meaningless because it allowed the voters no choice.
9. There was much activity in the town on election day.
10. Hitler and President Von Hindenberg personally saw to all the arrangements.
11. The story-teller's parents greeted people from time to time.
12. Heinz worked hard though he was only a little boy of ten.
13. Mother was a rather stupid woman who didn't understand anything.
14. Mother was shocked that Heinz was distributing sheets to everyone.

10. A Night with the Bears

On the night of January 11 a factory worker employed in the Civil Engineering Department of the Associated Cement Company's plant in Kymore near Dhariya village in Madhya Pradesh was trudging towards his masoor field. Most of Dhariya's 75 inhabitants had gone to sleep and everywhere was silence.

As Dangal walked, his mind went back to the days when in this very area, he had, with his shotgun, killed many wild marauding beasts on the prowl at night. However, for many years now the shotgun had lain unused, for when the Kymore plant had come up the threat from the wild beasts had receded. Today the only pests were the occasional straying cattle, the wild boar and the sambhar. Dangal was still lost in his reverie when he stepped into his masoor field and to what seemed certain, a gory death. 'Suddenly, a huge black mass loomed out of the darkness,' recounted Dangal later with a shudder. 'Six black bears snarled their fury at me. It was an awesome sight. It's a wonder I didn't faint, let alone die of fright at the prospect of being mauled to death by these beasts.'

'Even as I looked into the grizzly face of inevitable death, my instinct to survive was aroused. And I was determined to die fighting.'

Fortunately, Dangal didn't have time to ponder. The attack was sudden. The first bear reared on its hind legs and planted its forelegs on his shoulders. Dangal sprawled to the ground, the bear on top of him.

Then began his fight for life!

As death stared him in the face Dangal's first thought was of God. As he wrestled with 200 kilos of snarling fury, he prayed for a miracle.

Blood dripped from his shoulders, chest and legs, where sharp claws had taken a vicious toll. Then suddenly the initial mauling was over, and there was a respite. The bear lunged back, then leaped and skittered like a giant pup, pleased that it had won the first round. Or was it disappointment at the weak opposition from the man? But even as Dangal tottered to his feet, the snorting mouth and the gnashing teeth sounded the start of round two.

Dangal tensed. The hulking animal charged. And the two bodies merged in a bear hug. A searing pain in his chest numbed Dangal. But the foretaste of onrushing death jolted him with the horrible thought of the manner in which he was to die — his body torn to shreds, with the ever-hovering vultures to feast on the leftovers.

Dangal shuddered violently and resisted the brute pressure bearing him down. Shaking like a reed in the wind, he willed himself to stand up, staring at the awesome vision of death. One hand reached out to shield his throat from snarling teeth and lashing paws; with the other he strove to push back the beast.

Seeing the man still on his feet, two more bears from the pack — which had stood by snorting impatiently while their leader had first 'pickings' — plunged into the fray. One planted its forepaws on Dangal's shoulders seeking to rip his throat; the other bounded back, then leaped clear over his head just as he was borne to the ground again by the first bear's weight. What a fortunate fall that was, thought Dangal, as the whipping, thrusting paws of the leaping bear just grazed his chest and arms. Meanwhile, the other bear snapped and pawed at his body.

Dangal had begun to bleed profusely. Greatly weakened, his reactions had slowed down in the hideous game that was now on. For that's what it seemed as the animals, one after the other, played with the fallen man. All he could manage was to whisper a desperate prayer for help.

Perhaps it was the smell of the grizzly fur or the salty taste of his own blood — suddenly, with a loud animal-like bellow, Dangal rose and pounced on his nearest attacker, his left arm locking around its neck while with the other he wrenched at the fur and skin of its throat.

Dangal was almost transformed into an animal — his head was buried in the furry throat of the beast, his free arms and legs lashing out in savage fury. And from the bowels of the man came low, inhuman growls.

Then, in one last-ditch, convulsive effort, the enfeebled Dangal bit into the throat of the bear and lashed out in a ferocious heave, knocking the animal away from him. The effort was so great that he slipped and fell on a thorny bush.

Taken aback by the sudden ferocity of his attack, the bears paused in awe. They were stunned into immobility and Dangal, his spirits revived by the scent of victory, didn't go for the final kill. Instead he rose to his feet shakily and ran for the distant cover of the trees.

His lacerated body screamed for a soothing balm: his gored and shredded flesh almost nauseated him. Feeling dizzy, he fell down. But the low growling of the bears, cheated of their quarry, spurred him to renewed, desperate action. Stumbling to his feet, he wobbled from side to side, the thorny bushes rending further his flesh and garments. But Dangal was long past pain. His one thought, as he recalled, was to make it to his house, 'I must reach my folks before my lifeblood drains out ... They will take me to the Kymore hospital ... And then the doctors will save me ...'

This one thought urged him on in those final moments. Gasping for breath and barely alive, Dangal managed to reach home and fell into blessed unconsciousness against the door. He didn't see the shocked faces of his kinsfolk staring at his bloodied body. Nor did he hear their cries or queries. Gently, they lifted him onto a quickly improvised stretcher and hurried his mangled body to the hospital.

It was long past midnight when the unconscious Dangal (this time assisted by the doctor and his staff) began his struggle for life. Around 3.30 on Sunday morning the weary team finished patching up the torn mess that had been brought to them.

To colleagues, friends and relatives Dangal is a hero. His story will be told again and again with pride to the children of the village till it achieves folklore status. But for Dangal, every time he looks at the luscious pastures of his beloved fields, there will be haunting memories of a Saturday night and a Sunday morning.

(from *A night with the Bears* by Dom de Sa)

Glossary:

to maraud : to roam about raiding and looting.

to be on the prowl : to roam stealthily in search of prey.

to recede : to draw back; to become more distant.

reverie : day-dream.

recount : to tell what happened with all the details.

maul : to attack savagely and injure.

grizzly : grey-haired and old. A grizzly bear is a fierce North American bear.

instinct : that ability in living beings (animal and human) that tells them instantly, without the need to think, what to do and how to act in certain situations.

ponder :	to think over carefully
vicious :	cruel, evil
lunge:	a sudden thrust, a sudden forward movement of the body. 'To lunge' means to move the body suddenly forward.
gnashing teeth :	grinding teeth in anger
hulking :	big and clumsy
searing :	burning
to lacerate :	to tear into little pieces; to shred
nausea :	feeling of sickness in the stomach. 'To nauseate' means to cause this feeling.
quarry :	prey; victim

Vocabulary

A. Dangal had a foretaste of onrushing death which jolted him with the horirble thought of the manner in which he was to die.....

The prefix fore- means 'before'. Dangal had a taste of death before it had really come.

Use the prefix 'fore-' with the right form of these words to fill in the blanks.

most	*fathers*	*gather*	*see*	*finger*

1. The ____________ thought in everybody's mind was the safety of the children.
2. Nostradamus who lived in Europe in the 16th Century ____________ events that were to take place even in the 20th century.
3. The crowds had ____________ in the marketplace when they heard rumours that an open air play was to be performed there.
4. After the thumb comes the ____________ , and after that comes the middle finger which is the tallest of all the fingers.
5. Some of the customs that our ____________ followed in their time are still observed today.

B. *The prefix pre- is used when we talk about something before in time, position, rank or order.*
Add pre- to each of the words in the box.
Fill in the blanks in the sentences below with the new words.

-primary	*-natal*	*-historic*	*-professional*
-payment	*-determined*	*-mature*	

1. The dinosaurs lived before people existed. So there are no written or even oral records of these beasts. They lived in ______________ times.
2. At the hospital they were told that they must pay some money in advance. The hospital insisted on some ______________ .
3. They liked the hospital because it provided the medical care necessary for a mother before the birth of her child. The doctors believe that ______________ care is as important as ante-natal care.
4. The baby was born before its time, and so needed special attention. All ______________ babies do.
5. Before you join the engineering, medical or any other professional course, you will need to do a ______________ course of study.
6. He wanted to study music, but his grandfather's astrologer told him he had no choice in the matter. Fate had decided eveything for him. 'It's all ______________,' the astrologer said.
7. The youngest child who is about three years old goes to a ______________ school where she has toys to play with and picture books to look at.

C. The hulking animal charged.
'Charge' is one of those words which has more than one meaning.
In the sentence above, 'to charge' means 'to attack'. But what does 'charge' mean in these sentences? Choose the correct word from the three given in brackets.

1. They *charged* the man with murder.
   They (accused; convicted; acquitted) the man of murder.
2. The queen *charged* the elders to look after the princess.
   The queen (promised; requested; solemnly ordered) the elders to look after the princess.

3. The shopman *charged* Hari Rs. 280/- for the clock.
   The shopman (promised to pay Hari; asked Hari to pay; paid Hari) Rs. 280/- for the clock.
4. With a great bellow, the bull *charged at* the lion.
   With a great bellow, the bull (demanded money from; rushed at; ran away from) the lion.
5. As soon as Brigadier Gupta saw the headmistress, he *charged off* down the road.
   As soon as Brigadier Gupta saw the headmistress, he (shouted; shot her; ran off) down the road.

D. *Some words have two different meanings. Here are a few such words from the text. Which of the meanings, (a), (b) or (c), is closest to that applied in the text?*

1. gore:
   a. blood, especially blood that has been shed
   b. to pierce or wound with horns or tusks
2. toll:
   a. a tax or charge levied on those who use a particular service: e.g., when travelling by road in a bus or car you come across toll-gates where you have to pay a toll; the money thus collected is the tax and is used to maintain roads.
   b. When there is a war or riot and someone loses his life or limb we say that it is the toll he has paid. A toll is the cost one pays in life or limb or suffering in war, etc.
3. to skitter:
   a. to jump or dart about
   b. to skim along the surface of water
4. to rear:
   a. to rise up on hind legs
   b. to rear can also mean 'to bring up', e.g., a child or an animal
   c. (noun). The rear of an army is the end part of an army. The *rear* of a house is the back of the house.
5. spur:
   a. a small spiked or pointed wheel worn on the heel of a riding boot. This is used to urge a horse to run faster.
   b. a ridge sticking out or projecting from a mountain.

6. fray:
   a. (noun) a fight or a brawl
   b. (verb) to wear out into shreds. The collar of the shirt is frayed.

Comprehension

A. *Choose the correct ending (according to the text) to complete the sentences.*

1. Dangal had not used his gun for many years now because
   a. he rarely went out and didn't need it.
   b. there had not been any wild beasts seen in the area since the Kymore Cement factory's plant had come up.
   c. they had killed off all the wild beasts and there were none on the prowl any more.
   d. it was silent everywhere and the people were asleep.
2. He saw the bears
   a. even before he reached the masoor field.
   b. as he was on his way to the masoor field.
   c. as soon as he stepped into the masoor field.
   d. every day.
3. His immediate thought on seeing the animals was that
   a. he should have come here earlier.
   b. he must not die without a fight.
   c. he should have carried his gun.
   d. bears make excellent pets.
4. If he had time to ponder, perhaps
   a. the bears might have run.
   b. he would have been too frightened to fight back.
   c. he would never have stepped into the masoor field.
   d. he would have recited some beautiful poetry.
5. The furious bear
   a. prayed for a miracle.
   b. ripped Dangal's shoulders, chest and legs.
   c. started weeping bitterly.
   d. held out its hand and greeted him warmly.
6. After the first round the bear
   a. became tame as a pup.
   b. was dripping with blood.
   c. was very grieved at the weak opposition.
   d. prepared for the second.

7. Though Dangal was in great pain he fought on because
   a. he remembered his family who depended on him.
   b. he didn't want his body torn to shreds and left to be eaten up by vultures.
   c. he was not afraid of the bears.
   d. he loved fighting bears.
8. Dangal had to fight.
   a. more than one bear.
   b. only one bear.
   c. the bear and its mate.
   d. a very friendly bear.
9. In the end Dangal
   a. laughed at the joke.
   b. died.
   c. ran away.
   d. was rescued by his relatives.
10. The doctors managed to
   a. stitch up his torn and badly injured body.
   b. rouse Dangal from his unconscious state.
   c. give Dangal medicine.
   d. pay him for the trouble he had taken.

B. *Say whether the statements below are true or false according to the text. Mark them T if true, F if false and DS if the text doesn't say anything about it. Correct the ones that are false.*

1. Dangal didn't want to die without giving the bears a fight.
2. Dangal was a religious man and always prayed hard.
3. The bears had lain in wait for Dangal in the masoor field.
4. Dangal was transformed into an animal.
5. The bears had come into the village in search of food.
6. Dangal, though greatly enfeebled, managed to reach home.
7. Dangal will never forget the terrible night when he encountered the bears.
8. Dangal was in such terrible pain that his unconsciousness was like a blessing.
9. Dangal was cheated by the bears.
10. Dangal fell into the last ditch.
11. The doctors saved Dangal's life.
12. Everyone in the village talked about Dangal and praised him for his courage.

C. *Match the sentences in Column A with those with the same meaning in Column B.*

Column A	Column B
1. The terrible grey old face (of the bear) was like the face of death — death which is certain and inescapable.	a. The bears paused in awe. They were stunned into immobility and Dangal, his spirits revived by the scent of victory, didn't go for the final kill. Instead he rose to his feet shakily and ran for the distant cover of the trees.
2. The tale of Dangal's fight with the bears will one day become part of the collection of stories people remember and tell their children and grandchildren.	b. A huge black mass loomed out of the darkness.
3. The animals were surprised into inaction. But Dangal, though heartened by the bears' defeat, tottered to his feet and tried to hide behind some trees in the distance.	c. But the low growling of the bears, cheated of their quarry, spurred him to renewed, desperate action.
4. Even in his weakened condition Dangal roused himself suddenly and made one final desperate attempt to beat back the bear. He dug his teeth into the bear's throat and hit out savagely, pushing the brute down and away from him.	d. The grizzly face of inevitable death.
5. A great dark form appeared menacingly out of the blackness of the night.	e. His story will be told again and again with pride to the children of the village till it achieves folklore status.
6. The fearful creatures, enraged at having lost their prey, made angry, rumbling noises. This was enough for Dangal who got up and ran.	f. Then, in one last-ditch, convulsive effort, the enfeebled Dangal bit into the throat of the bear and lashed out in a ferocious heave, knocking the animal away from him.

11. Ziré Buzette

Maurice des Ombriaux was born in Hainault, Belgium, in 1868. Like many other Belgian writers, he loved the countryside; and there he has placed the story of Ziré Buzette. The French-speaking Belgians, of whom he was one, are able to laugh at life more sincerely than their Fleming cousins, and the humour of this short piece cannot fail to bring a smile to the reader's lips.

For many years Ziré Buzette had coughed his soul out, one of those hard dry coughs which seem to shake and tear the chest and make those who hear it say, 'He has not long to live.'

It was true. For a long time already Ziré Buzette had not had long to live.

He was a plasterer during the summer, and he was seen going out early in the morning with his bucket, brushes and sleeves, coughing all the time.

'Poor Ziré Buzette,' said everyone. 'To do that sort of thing with his health! It is the lime that eats away his lungs. No, he has not long to live.'

'That miserable Ziré Buzette, how brave he is! Nothing will persuade him to go into the hospital. He insists on working, and all the time his blood is being poisoned. He won't last long, that's certain.'

And Ziré went off to make the house beautiful with whitewash, coughing on his ladder, with a face as white as his apron. He used to whitewash kitchens and rooms too, and everyone looked after him through sympathy. For pity, and because his prices were moderate, he was given work everywhere, and his services were demanded a long time ahead. Even in the humblest cottages a piece of meat was put in the oven for him.

'That poor Ziré Buzette!' they said. 'He needs strengthening. He is worn out. He won't last long.'

In the farms he was made to drink a mouthful of good wine everyday. He needed it, too, not having long to live!

Yet Zire Buzette still lived on, and on Sundays he even played the violin for young people to dance. While he played it, he coughed.

'Poor Ziré Buzette, he must be very poor if he has to get cold sitting out during a whole evening with such an illness. He has no strength in his blood. It makes your heart ache to see him shivering and coughing. Ah, no indeed, he won't last long!'

And so, at every pause, he was offered a good drink and also slices of cake. It was the least that one could do for this miserable wreck, who had not long to live. And he was liked as a musician, nobody could make people dance as he could. He played so well that even those with clumsy feet, even the beginners went to dance and needed no persuasion. The leaders of the parties arranged with him from the beginning of the year to be quite sure that he would not fail them.

How he was spoiled! How he was 'treated!' For his sake a barrel of beer was placed on the musician's platform. Good old Ziré Buzette must be well looked after, for he would not play much longer, and who would make them all dance then?

Ziré Buzette never refused anything, drank everything and ate everything slowly, without ever hurrying himself. To see him thus one would not have said that he had not long to live.

'It's his disease,' they thought. 'He needs food, poor fellow. Yes, one may well say so; and in spite of that he has not long to live.'

Ziré also went to the big houses of the neighbourhood to make the young people dance at parties, and everywhere he was treated better than a workman or a servant. He was regarded almost as a friend. I do not know what else to say except that he had not long to live.

In winter no whitewashing was done and so, to earn his living, and to occupy his leisure, Ziré Buzette, still coughing, became a shoemaker. He was not, truth to tell, remarkably capable at this trade, but work never failed him. People ordered slippers from him and he made boots for children. 'Poor Ziré Buzette! He must live. It is a duty to give him work. He will not last long.'

Weak and sick, perpetually coughing, Ziré Buzette, who had not long to live, had nevertheless already buried two wives. His first had married him out of pity, it was said. 'Let us risk it,' she had thought. 'It does not bind me to much: he will not last long.'

She died of a chill.

The second had married him for his money, which was not much. 'It is a good business,' she thought, 'I have nothing, and as he will not last long I shall inherit from him. Then I can find whom I like after him.'

She died.

And now the rumour spread through the village that he was going to be married again, for the third time, to a girl who was only twenty years of age.

'Did you ever hear of such a thing!' asked the gossips. 'He has not long to live, in any case.'

'There is one who has an eye on his house and orchard,' said others. 'How shameful! She knows well enough that he won't last long.'

Ziré Buzette had his little house and piece of ground surrounded by the property of the Brothers Blairaux, the richest people in the village. One was mayor, another farmer, the third treasurer of the Charity Organization, and all three were bachelors. Big strong fellows, with powerful limbs, they looked as if they were made to live a hundred years. They owned over a hundred acres of land and bought more every year. It was said that half the village belonged to them. Their farm, field, garden and orchard made a splendid place. It was the finest property in the village. It had cost them a great deal of money and trouble. They had had to buy a bit of land from one, a ruined cottage from another, a hut here, a building there. They pulled down, filled up, levelled the ground. In order that the estate might be complete and perfect, they only needed Ziré Buzette's cottage.

'He won't last long,' they said to themselves. 'We shall have it for nothing on his death.'

But their wish finally became stronger than their reason. They wanted to have the estate at once, as soon as possible; for perhaps after Ziré's death his heirs might make difficulties. Their demands might be immoderate.

After all sorts of village tricks, they started negotiations with Ziré Buzette. But their cunning plans were of no use; he would not sell. He shook his head with its pale face and said, coughing, 'Ask me anything else, sirs; but do not ask me to leave the house of my grandfathers. You know I have not long to live. Be patient, I won't go anywhere else for the short time that is left to me. I will die in the house where I was born and where all my people have died.'

He met the pressing requests of his neighbours with a gentle obstinacy. There was nothing to be done; he remained resolute. They tried in vain to frighten him with threats. They stopped dealing with him, and the mayor engaged another musician for the village festival. Ziré Buzette felt wounded by this blow, and all the villagers took his part and refused to go to the village dance. They were angry with the mayor. 'Treat a poor fellow in that way, when he has not long to live! You must be heartless!'

The Brothers Blairaux, to avoid danger, made peace with him. They increased their offers, but Ziré still refused. 'I want to die in my father's house,' he said.

'Sell it to us and you shall keep the use of it during your lifetime,' said the treasurer of the Charity Organization, who thought that Ziré Buzette would not last long. The idea pleased the plasterer; they discussed it and finally agreed. Ziré Buzette was to retain the use of the cottage until his death, and the Blairaux would have it then. They would also pay him rent while he lived — 'but only once or twice at most, for Ziré would not last long.'

And the whole village said, 'Those Blairaux are fine foxes. They've bought Zire's place cheaply; for he won't last long.'

Every year Ziré got his rent, and each time the Blairaux thought they had paid for the last time.

The mayor died without having seen the orchard joined to his land. The two other brothers paid the proper amount next time with sad faces. Then the farmer died, and Ziré, who had not long to live, continued coughing and drawing his rent. He had already received two or three times the value of his field, but the people said that this Blairaux was a lucky fellow.

A mad desire to choke the life out of the plasterer's throat made Blairaux's fingers tremble every time he had to hand over the precious gold pieces. 'Ah! There you are! Are you never going to die!' he used to say.

'Monsieur Blairaux, how can you say such things to a poor man like me, who has not long to live,' answered Ziré, coughing.

He buried the third Blairaux and then died himself, over a hundred years old. For over three-quarters of a century he had not had long to live.

(from *Stories from Many Lands* by Maurice Des Ombriaux)

Glossary

apron :	cloth or leather covering worn in front of the body to protect the clothes
wreck :	ruin; something seriously damaged; a broken down, sickly person
perpetually :	continually, never stopping; continuing indefinitely; forever; for a life time
nevertheless :	even so; all the same
rumour :	an unconfirmed story — a report or a piece of news passed on from person to person and often believed, whether it is true or not
a gossip :	a person who goes about gathering and spreading rumours and local news
to gossip :	to talk idly
negotiations :	business discussions
obstinacy :	stubborness; persistence
sleeve :	the part of the garment which covers the arm. (Zire Buzette wore a sleeve — an extra sleeve on top of his coat or shirt sleeve to protect it from getting dirty.)

Vocabulary

A. *In Box B are words for parts of the human body. Add 'd' or 'ed' to each of these and join it with its matching word in Box A using a hyphen to make a new sensible compound word. e.g. dark-haired.,*

Box A

dark —	*long* —	*full* —	*broad* —
smooth —	*short* —	*tight* —	*straight* —
swift —	*curly* —	*thin* —	*square* —
strong —	*kind* —	*snub* —	*large* —
iron —	*evil* —	*hawk* —	*quick* —
weak —	*grey* —	*light* —	*round* —
flat —	*wavy* —		

Box B

__*back*	__*cheek*	__*ear*	__*hair*	__*jaw*
__*blood*	__*face*	__*eye*	__*hand*	__*knee*
__*bone*	__*throat*	__*finger*	__*head*	__*leg*
__*nose*	__*shoulder*	__*flesh*	__*neck*	__*lip (ped)*
__*foot*	__*mind*	__*tongue*	__*chest*	__*mouth*

B. *In the passage below the verbs have all been substituted with the word 'glob' (Some of the verbs are made up of two words but have only one 'glob' to represent the two words.) The adjectives in the passage have been substituted with the word 'zog'.*

Find the correct verbs and adjectives and rewrite this passage. (There may of course be more than one correct verb or adjective.)

Zoggy one morning in a zogged street of a suburb, there globbed a lady and a boy of four. The boy globbed zog and zog, the lady globbed in her zogginess and globbed zogly at her son. The boy globbing a hoop, a zog, zog, zog one. He globbed after it zogly, globbing his zog knees and globbing his stick. It globbed not at all necessary to glob the stick so glob, but that glob what he globbed.

C. *You can change many adjectives and a few nouns into verbs by adding the suffix* *-en* *e.g.* That poor Zire Buzette, He needs <u>strengthening</u>. *Complete the sentences given below. The first one has been done for you.*

1. This road is too narrow for all the traffic. It needs to be made wide. This road needs to be ______________ ed,

   or

   This road needs ______________ ing.
2. The pit you've dug is too shallow. It should be made deeper. It should be ______________ ed.
3. There was a shadow which made the whole picture dark. There was a shadow which ______________ ed the whole picture.
4. Put in some more sugar into the mixture. It needs to be made sweeter.
   It needs to be ______________ ed.

5. The boy was embarrassed. He became red.
   His face ______________ ed.
6. You can make your burden lighter by using thermocole instead of paper.
   You can ______________ your burden by using thermocole.

Comprehension

A. *Tick off the correct endings to the sentences below:*

1. Everybody in the village pitied Zire Buzette because they thought
   a. he was starving.
   b. he was going to die very soon.
   c. he needed strengthening.
   d. his prices were moderate.
2. Zire's second wife hoped that
   a. he would teach her to play the violin.
   b. she would be able to nurse him back to health.
   c. they would have a long and happy married life together.
   d. she would get all his money when he died.
3. Zire's first wife
   a. caught a cold and died because of it.
   b. buried two wives.
   c. was perpetually coughing.
   d. was passionately in love with him.
3. Zire's second wife
   a. spread rumours in the village that he was going to be married again.
   b. was only twenty years old.
   c. played the violin beautifully.
   d. thought he would not last long.
5. It was rumoured in the village that
   a. Zire had inherited his wife's property.
   b. he was going to marry for the third time.
   c. he had died.
   d. he was going to buy the mayor's house.
6. Zire Buzette was
   a. an excellent shoemaker.
   b. a popular violinist.
   c. a greedy old miser.
   d. a scheming village politician.

7. The Blairaux brothers
   a. hated the sight of Zire.
   b. earned their living by whitewashing houses.
   c. had their eyes on Zire Buzette.
   d. were ill and needed strength-giving food.
8. Zire Buzette didn't die
   a. until he had earned a lot of money.
   b. until he was well over a hundred years old.
   c. because he was a hard-working man.
   d. though everyone tried to do away with him.

B. *Mark the true statements T the false one F and the ones about which the story doesn't say anything DS. Correct the false statements.*

1. Zire Buzette looked healthy and strong.
2. The villagers hoped he would die so that they could get his property.
3. None of the three Blairaux brothers was married.
4. The Blairaux brothers owned a lot of land in the village.
5. The mayor, the farmer and the treasurer of the charity organisation hoped that they would get Zire Buzette's cottage for nothing when he died.
6. When the Blairaux brothers approached Buzette with their proposal to buy his house he was delighted and agreed immediately.
7. Buzette outlived his three wives.
8. When the Blairaux brother stopped dealing with him the villagers took Buzette's side.
9. Buzette collected rent from the Blairaux brothers as long as they were alive.
10. After the Blairaux brothers died Buzette collected rent from their heirs.
11. Buzette must have attended a great many funerals during his life.
12. The Blairaux brothers didn't like parting with their money to Buzette.

C. *Give one, two or at the most three word answers to each question below. Time yourself if you want to.*

1. What was Zire Buzette's profession?
2. What did Zire Buzette often get to eat?

3. What did he get to drink?
4. What did he wear when he went to work?
5. Who were his nearest neighbours?
6. Where had he got his house from?
7. What did he make during summer?
8. How many wives did he outlive?
9. What did the Blairaux brothers pay him?
10. How old do you think Zire Buzette could have been when he finally died?

C. *In Box A there are some idiomatic expressions taken from the text. Match them with their correct meaning given in Box B.*

Box A

1. *It is the lime that eats away his lungs!*
2. *It was the least one could do for this miserable wreck who had not long to live.*
3. *... but work never failed him.*
4. *Poor fellow, he won't last long.*
5. *Weak and sick, perpetually coughing, Zire Buzette who had not long to live had nevertheless already buried two wives.*
6. *He is worn out.*
7. *It makes your heart ache to see him shivering and coughing.*
8. *The leaders of the parties arranged with him from the beginning of the year to be quite sure that he would not fail them.*

Box B

a. *always helped him in time of need*
b. *corrodes, destroys by corroding*
c. *completely tired; exhausted*
d. *would stand by them / would not let them down / would not disappoint them*
e. *would die soon*
f. *make you very, very unhappy*
g. *had outlived*
h. *one couldn't do less than this*

12. The Tunguska Event

This passage is taken from the book 'Cosmos' in which the writer Carl Sagan talks about a strange phenomenon that occured in Tunguska, Central Siberia, in the year 1908. The Revolution had not ended and Russia was still under the rule of the Czar at the time of the Tunguska event.

The Earth is a more or less placid place. Things change, but slowly. We can lead a full life and never personally encounter a natural disaster more violent than a storm. And so we become complacent, relaxed, unconcerned. But in the history of nature, the record is clear. Worlds have been devastated. Even we humans have made our own disasters: some of these have been inadvertent, while others have been intentional. Even in our own century bizarre natural events have occurred. One of these events is the Tunguska Event. In the early morning hours of June 30, 1908, in Tunguska, Central Siberia, a giant fireball was seen moving rapidly across the sky. Where it touched the horizon, an enormous explosion took place. It levelled some 2,000 square kilometres of forest and burned thousands of trees in a flash fire near the impact site. It produced an atmospheric shock-wave that twice circled the earth. For two days afterwards, there was so much fine dust in the atmosphere that one could read a newspaper at night by the scattered light, in the streets of London, 10,000 kilometres away.

Ten years after the Russian Revolution an expedition arrived at the Tunguska site to examine the ground and interview the witnesses. Here are some of the accounts they brought back:

Early in the morning when everyone was asleep in the tent, it was blown up into the air, together with the occupants. When they fell back to earth, the whole family suffered slight bruises, but Akulina and Ivan actually lost consciousness. When they regained it they heard a great deal of noise and saw the forest blazing round them and much of it devastated.

I was sitting in the porch of the house at the trading station of Vanovara at breakfast time and looking towards the north, when suddenly ... the sky split in two, and high above the forest the whole northern part of the sky appeared to be covered with fire. At that moment I felt a great heat as if my shirt had caught fire ... I wanted to pull off my shirt and throw it away, but at that moment there was a bang in the sky, and a mighty crash was heard. I was thrown on the ground some distance away from the porch and for a moment I lost consciousness. My wife ran out and carried me into the hut. The crash was followed by a noise like stones falling from the sky, or guns firing. The earth trembled, and when I lay on the ground I covered my head because I was afraid that stones might hit it. At the moment when the sky opened, a hot wind, as from a cannon, blew past the huts from the north. It left its mark on the ground ...

When I sat down to have my breakfast beside my plough, I heard sudden bangs, as if from gun-fire. My horse fell to its knees. From the north side above the forest a flame shot up ... Then I saw that the fir forest had been bent over by the wind and I thought of a hurricane. I seized hold of my plough with both hands, so that it would not be carried away. The wind was so strong that it carried off some of the soil from the surface of the ground, and then the hurricane drove a wall of water up the Angara. I saw it all quite clearly, because my land was on a hillside.

The roar frightened the horses to such an extent that some galloped off in panic, dragging the ploughs in different directions, and others collapsed.

The carpenters, after the first and second crashes had crossed themselves in stupefaction, and when the third crash resounded they fell backwards from the building onto the chips of wood. Some of them were so stunned and utterly terrified that I had to calm them down and reassure them. We all abandoned work and went into the village. There, whole crowds of local inhabitants were gathered in the streets in terror, talking about this phenomenon.

I was in the fields ... and had only just got one horse harnessed to the harrow and begun to attach another when suddenly I heard what sounded like loud shots to the right. I immediately turned round and saw an elongated flaming object flying through the sky. The front part was much broader than the tail end and its colour was like fire in the day-time. It was many times bigger than the sun but much dimmer, so that it was possible to look at it with the naked eye. Behind the flames trailed what looked like dust. It was wreathed in little puffs, and blue streamers were left behind from the flames ... As soon as the flame had disappeared, bangs louder than shots from a gun were heard, the ground could be felt to tremble, and the window panes in the cabin were shattered.

... I was washing wool on the bank of the River Kan. Suddenly a noise like the fluttering of the wings of a frightened bird was heard ... and a kind of swell came up the river. After this came a single sharp bang so loud that one of the workmen ... . fell into the water.

This remarkable occurrence is called the Tunguska Event. According to some scientists it was caused by a piece of comet hitting the earth.

(from *Cosmos, the story of Cosmic evolution, Science and Civilization*
by Carl Sagan)

Comets

What could have caused the terrible explosion called the Tunguska Event? Astronomers tell us that in the vast spaces between the planets there are many objects, some composed partly of organic molecules. They range from grains of dust to irregular blocks the size of Nicaragua or Bhutan. And sometimes, by accident, there is a planet in the way. The Tunguska Event was probably caused, says Sagan, by an icy cometary fragment about a hundred metres across — the size of a football field — weighing a million tons, moving at about thirty kilometres per second, 70,000 miles per hour. The flashes were caused by the impact of a small asteroid or a piece of a comet.

A comet is made mostly of ice — water (H_2O) ice, with a little methane (CH_4) ice, and some ammonia (NH_2) ice. Striking the Earth's atmosphere, a modest cometary fragment would produce a great radiant fireball and a mighty blast wave, which would burn trees, level forests and be heard around the world. But it might not make much of a crater in the ground. The ices would all be melted during entry. There would be few recognizable pieces of the comet left — perhaps only a smattering of small grains from the non-icy parts of the cometary nucleus. Recently, the Soviet scientist E. Sobotovich has identified a large number of tiny diamonds strewn over the Tunguska site. Such diamonds are already known to exist in meteorites that have survived impact, and that may originate ultimately from comets.

On many a clear night, if you look patiently up at the sky, you will see a solitary meteor blazing briefly overhead. On some nights you can see a shower of meteors, always on the same few days of every year — a natural fireworks display, an entertainment in the heavens. These meteors are made by tiny grains, smaller than a mustard seed. They are less shooting stars than falling fluff. Momentarily brilliant as they enter the Earth's atmosphere, they are heated and destroyed by friction at a height of about 100 kilometres. Meteors are the remnants of comets. Old comets, heated by repeated passages near the Sun, break up, evaporate and disintegrate. The debris

   c. exploded.
   d. was blown up into the air together with it.

9. The person washing wool on the river bank
   a. saw a frightened bird fluttering its wings.
   b. heard a noise which sounded like the fluttering of a bird's wings.
   c. heard a swell coming up the river.
   d. fell into the water.

10. Some of the witnesses who were interviewed spoke about
    a. the behaviour of animals.
    b. why they lived in Siberia.
    c. what action the government should take.
    d. the duty of the citizens.

B. *Some of the statements given below are true according to the text, and some are not true; there are a few others about which the text doesn't say anything. Mark T against the statements that are true; F against those that are false and DS against those about which the text does not say anything. Correct the statements that are not true.*

1. Many bizarre events which have taken place on earth have made an impact on other planets.
2. The Tunguska Event had an impact over an area far greater than its actual site.
3. The people who witnessed the Tunguska Event were all poor villagers.
4. Events of this kind are the result of God's anger.
5. One of the witnesses of the Tunguska Event, washing wool on the bank of River Kan, heard a frightened bird.
6. Many people were killed at the Tunguska site.
7. Most of the people who gave their accounts of the Tunguska Event had died in the explosion.
8. One person said that his shirt had caught fire.
9. Another person said that stones fell from the sky, making a loud noise.
10. Because his land was on a hillside, one man was able to see what happened very clearly.

Other anthologies from Orient Longman

The Refugee and Other Stories

edited by A.A. Balakrishnan and A. George

Stories by K.A. Abbas, P.G. Wodehouse, Will P. Jenkins, Norah Burke, Katherine Mansfield, O. Henry, Sarat Chandra Chatterjee and D.H. Lawrence, with appropriate notes and exercises for college students.

Let's Go Home and Other Stories

edited by Meenakshi Mukherjee

A remarkable collection of short stories by eminent Indian writers, including R.K. Narayan, Mulk Raj Anand, Khushwant Singh and Ruskin Bond.

Statements — An anthology of Indian prose in English

edited by Adil Jussawalla and Eunice de Souza

An unusual, stimulating anthology with something important to say on problems of interest and concern in India today.

The Living Language

edited by C.K. Narayanan

A collection of fourteen essays giving consideration to the reputation of the essayist and the relevance of the theme, providing a faithful reflection ~ the mood of the time. The essays include those by Bertrand Russell, Aldous Huxley, R.K. Narayan, Jawaharlal Nehru, Jacob Bronowski, C.V. Raman and others.